KIMO'S HERO

BROTHERHOOD PROTECTORS HAWAII
BOOK EIGHT

ELLE JAMES

TWISTED PAGE INC

ISBN EBOOK: 978-1-62695-658-2

ISBN PAPERBACK: 978-1-62695-641-4

ISBN HARDCOVER: 978-1-62695-691-9

For my Mike and Nora, my travel buddies who helped me brainstorm the ending and for all the years of adventures.

For Yorkies who make me get out of my writing chair a hundred times a day.
Elle James

AUTHOR'S NOTE

Enjoy other military books by Elle James

Brotherhood Protectors Hawaii
Kalea's Hero (#1)
Leilani's Hero (#2)
Kiana's Hero (#3)
Casey's Hero (#4)
Maliea's Hero (#5)
Emi's Hero (#6)
Sachie's Hero (#7)
Kimo's Hero (#8)
Alana's Hero (#9)

Visit ellejames.com for more titles and release dates
Join her newsletter at
https://ellejames.com/contact/

KIMO'S HERO

BROTHERHOOD PROTECTORS
HAWAII BOOK #8

New York Times & USA Today
Bestselling Author

ELLE JAMES

CHAPTER 1

"READY?" Alana gave Kimo a thumbs-up.

"Ready." Kimo Kekoa returned the gesture, adjusted the regulator in her mouth, held onto her mask and her camera and tipped backward off the dive boat into the inky-black waters of the ocean.

As soon as she sank beneath the surface, she breathed air from the scuba tank, righted herself in the water and kicked her flippers, sending her away from the dive boat they'd anchored off the shore of Maui.

The night dive was for the specific purpose of capturing the beauty of bioluminescence. The moonless sky and the warmth of summer made the night perfect. Already, they'd seen the eerie blue-green glow of the tiny plankton lighting up the shoreline.

As soon as Alana swam up beside Kimo, they dove deeper and swam nearer to the shore, hoping to get photos of marine life with the backdrop of the blue glow.

No sooner had they dove downward, swimming toward the shore, than a turtle swam up from the ocean floor. While Alana shined an LED light, Kimo aimed her underwater camera at the turtle, catching the image.

The turtle, apparently curious, circled Kimo and Alana for several minutes, giving them every angle to capture the free-flowing beauty of the creature before it swam away.

Kimo's viewfinder followed until the turtle disappeared into the darkness.

A hand on her arm made her turn toward her friend.

Alana pointed toward a rocky reef. Movement drew their attention to the camouflaged legs of an octopus, clinging to mottled gray rocks.

Kimo swam closer, snapping more photographs, excited to add the octopus to their shoot.

When the octopus slipped through a crevice, disappearing out of sight, Alana and Kimo rose above the rocks, searching for their next subject.

Colorful fish flitted past them. Again, Alana shined the light while Kimo photographed, at times, capturing the blue haze of the bioluminescence in the background.

After they'd been underwater for forty-five minutes, never going much deeper than twenty or thirty feet, Kimo motioned to Alana, tapping her dive watch.

Alana nodded, gave the OK sign and swam over the top of a reef, heading toward the dive boat, shining her light into the cracks and crevices of the jagged rocks.

Kimo swam alongside her friend, camera at the ready. It never failed that when she set it aside, some of the most spectacular sights appeared, whether they were fish, turtles or other marine life, and by the time she raised her camera again, they'd be gone.

This time, Alana's light bounced off straight, parallel lines on the other side of the shallow reef. Straight lines weren't natural in this environment where varied shapes of rocks, coral and seaweed should have been.

Kimo and Alana exchanged glances. Both women shrugged and then moved closer.

Once they cleared the reef, a large parrotfish swam past them. Kimo focused on the colorful fish, snapping a stream of photos of it as it swam away. Beyond the parrotfish, a shipping container appeared, settled onto the sandy surface of the ocean floor.

As Kimo neared the container, she saw the door was slightly ajar, but not enough to see inside.

Kimo grabbed the door and tried to push it wider. It didn't budge.

With the oxygen nearly gone in her tank, she

shook her head and motioned for Alana to ascend. Alana checked her gauge, nodded and started up.

Kimo dropped a pin on her dive watch's GPS, marking the spot, and followed Alana to the surface.

They emerged, not far from their boat, swam over, slung their flippers over the side and climbed the ladder.

"That was amazing," Alana exclaimed. "Those photos of the turtle and the octopus will be great for the dive brochures. Still, I'm curious about that shipping container."

"Me, too." Kimo pulled off her mask and snorkel, shrugged out of her buoyancy control device and set it, with the tank, on the deck. She helped Alana out of hers, then straightened.

The steady blue glow of bioluminescence lit the ocean near the reef and shoreline, filling Kimo with her own wonder and amazement. "It's beautiful."

Alana stood beside her. "We picked a perfect night for this."

Kimo nodded in the faint glow cast by the required lights affixed to the bow and stern of the small boat. "Thanks for coming with me when I'm sure you'd rather be with your fiancé."

Alana draped an arm over her friend's shoulder. "How often do we get to witness such a colorful display of nature? I have the rest of my life to spend with Vance. I can spare a night of diving with my dear friend, especially when we're treated to such an impressive display." She let her arm fall to her side. "So, are we done, or are we going back down for more impressive shots?"

"If you're up for it, I'd like to go down for a little longer. Maybe take a pry bar and look inside that container."

"I'm up for it and curious as well," Alana said.

"I just want to download what I have onto my laptop first."

"And while you download," Alana said, "I'll switch tanks."

Kimo smiled at her friend. "Great. I won't be long. Hopefully, we can be back on shore by midnight."

"Sounds like a plan," Alana said. "I might even get a good night's sleep before Vance and I meet with the wedding planner to go over wedding venues."

Kimo frowned. "You're meeting with her tomorrow?"

Alana sighed. "She insists. If I had it my way, I'd be satisfied with a small ceremony in front of a justice of the peace. Vance is the one insisting on a venue and all the things."

"Speaking of wedding planners, why didn't you go with Kalea's friend, Casey, for a wedding planner?"

"You know I love Kalea, but she's on the Big Island, Casey's on Oahu and Kinsley is the sister of Vance's friend here on Maui. Plus, Vance is paying for the planner and the venue."

"You realize it's your wedding, too," Kimo reminded her friend.

"Yeah, but neither one of us has been married before. I figure if Vance wants a fancy wedding, he deserves one."

"Did you tell him you didn't want a big wedding?"

"When he first asked. But he was so excited about planning. I didn't have the heart to tell him it was more than I wanted."

"You should, you know."

"It doesn't matter that much to me as long as I don't have to do all the work. Since he hired a wedding planner, I won't have to worry about all the fine details. Kinsley has it all under control." Alana removed the regulator, unclamped the tank and removed it from her BCD. She replaced it with a full tank, tightened the strap and locked it in place. "We just have to tell her a few of our preferences and off she goes to make it happen." She straightened and grinned. "You still going to be one of my bride's maids?"

"Of course," Kimo laid a towel across her damp legs, settled the laptop on it and booted the hard drive. Once the screen blinked to life, she down-loaded the images from her camera onto the computer and cloud.

By the time she was done, Alana had the second BCD loaded with a fresh tank. She glanced across at Kimo, one corner of her mouth quirking upward.

"We've known each other for a long time, but I'll never understand why your name is Kimo," Alana said. "It's typically a male child's name in Hawaiian."

Kimo snorted. "It's simple. My father was so proud of his first and only child's birth, he blessed me with the name, gender be damned. I weathered some kidding as a child, but it didn't bother me. My folks loved me and I loved them."

Alana shook her head. "Actually, you're a complete badass, so the name fits."

Kimo grinned. "Thanks." She slid the laptop into its case, shoved it into her backpack and placed it on the shelf near the helm alongside the fire extinguisher and radio. She sorted through the tool cubby until she found a metal pry bar and laid it on a bench.

When she turned, Alana held up her BCD and helped her slip it over her shoulders. Kimo buckled it in place and helped Alana into hers. She pulled her mask and snorkel over her face. After a quick glance at her gauges and an air test, she grabbed the pry bar, laid it on the rear platform and sat beside it. Kimo tugged her flippers over her feet, picked up her camera and waited for Alana.

"Ready?" Alana asked, flashlight strap looped around her wrist. She held up the pry bar. "I'll take the pry bar."

Kimo nodded, held onto her mask with one hand and the camera on the selfie stick with the other.

Then, she pushed off the back platform, sliding into the water.

Using the pinned location, Kimo led the way with Alana at her side, shining the flashlight at the ocean floor ahead of them.

They arrived fairly quickly.

Alana handed the flashlight to Kimo and applied the pry bar to the container door.

Kimo understood shipping containers sometimes slid off cargo ships during storms. This one could have done the same. However, most cargo ships didn't come this close to shore. She was curious about its contents. If it had been there long, the contents could have disintegrated unless it was made of plastic, glass or something equally resistant to erosive effects of warm salt water.

Alana jammed the pry bar into the narrow gap between the door and the side of the container and fought for a way to lean into the metal bar without floating away from it. She planted her feet against the side of the box, gripped the bar and pulled while pushing the box with her feet. The weightless effect of the water didn't give her much leverage, but the door moved slightly, displacing the sand in its way.

Kimo hurried forward and slid her foot across the sand in an attempt to clear the path the door must take to open.

Another attempt, pulling back on the bar without as much sand in the way, allowed the door to open another three inches before bogging down in the sand.

Alana lowered the bar and swam backward, allowing Kimo to move close enough to shine the flashlight into the box.

Kimo shined the light into the container, trying to make out shapes in the murky water stirred up by the sand. Fish rushed toward her, in a frantic hurry to escape the interior.

When the sand slowly settled, blurred shapes cleared. If she hadn't had a regulator in her mouth, Kimo would have gasped. Her heart leaped and hammered against her chest.

Inside the box were at least half a dozen semi-decomposed bodies—people whose wrists had been shackled to the sides of the metal container.

Her stomach heaved, and her hand shook so badly she dropped the flashlight.

Alana bent to retrieve it and edged around Kimo to shine the beam into the box.

She stiffened beside Kimo. She dropped the pry bar, and her hand shot out to clutch Kimo's arm.

Her heart pounding hard against her ribs, Kimo automatically raised the camera perched on the selfie stick, stuck it through the opening, and pressed the button, snapping several photographs before she touched Alana's hand and pointed upward.

Without hesitation, Alana kicked her flippers, sending herself rising toward the surface.

As Kimo hurried to catch up, the hum of a motor rumbled in her ears.

They hadn't left the dive boat running, which meant another boat was in the area.

Alana slowed the speed of her ascent as if remembering to rise with the bubbles, not ahead of them. Though they hadn't been very deep for long, decompression sickness was real and dangerous.

Kimo kept her ascent steady, the rumble of the motor growing increasingly louder as Alana neared the surface.

Kimo was three body lengths behind Alana when the other woman crested.

A spotlight shone from the edge of a boat cut low to the surface, barely visible in the night. The beam found and held Alana as she raised her hand to wave for help.

Instead of slowing, the boat driver increased its speed, aiming straight for Alana, while the spotlight continued to track her in the water.

Alana backpaddled in an attempt to sink below the surface. She barely managed to sink beneath the surface just in time for the boat to race over her exact location.

Kimo couldn't tell from her position if Alana had gone deep enough to avoid being struck.

Hit or not, the force of the displaced water spun Alana around and back toward the surface, following the trajectory of the motorboat, and taking her further from where Kimo had come up.

The boat made a rapid turn and headed back toward Alana.

Kimo swam toward her friend as fast as she could but was too far to get to her in time.

The spotlight found Alana again. Someone on the craft extended a boat hook, snagged Alana's gear and dragged her toward the boat.

No.

Kimo's heart squeezed hard in her chest as she swam toward her friend. Alana's limp body was dragged aboard the boat.

Dear God. Was she hurt? Was she dead?

The spotlight shifted from Alana to the water surrounding the boat.

"There has to be another diver," a voice called out over the sound of the engine. "Find him. We can't afford loose ends."

When Kimo heard the words, she stopped swimming toward the boat.

The spotlight's beam swept over the smooth surface of the ocean, moving ever closer to her position.

As if mesmerized by the beam, Kimo froze until the light struck her eyes, blinding her.

"There!" a man shouted.

"Get him!" another voice echoed across the water.

The boat's engine revved. The bow spun around

as the man holding the spotlight shifted to keep the beam on her.

Her pulse spiking, Kimo swam backward. They were coming for her.

As the craft completed the turn and started for her, she tucked and dove beneath the surface, kicking her flippers hard, sending herself as deep as she could get—out of the way of the boat and its propellers.

She swam as fast as she could, going deeper and deeper. The boat slowed over her. The spotlight searched the water, found her and tracked her movement.

Kimo couldn't go deeper. The ocean's sandy floor was barely twenty feet down. The clear water did little to hide her. She had to find cover, somewhere to hide.

Darkness rose ahead of her.

The reef.

She kicked hard, aiming for the jagged rocks.

The boat's muffled motor rumbled overhead. A popping sound reached her ears, and something shiny pierced the water, zipping past her head so fast she couldn't tell what it was. When another small, shiny object whizzed past the opposite side of her head, her blood chilled.

Bullets. They were shooting at her.

With the reef just ahead of her, she pushed harder, faster, flicking her flippers.

If she could reach the reef, the boat driver would

be foolish to follow. She could hide among the jagged, volcanic rocks.

More bullets penetrated the water around her. Something stung her calf, but she didn't slow. Couldn't, if she wanted to live.

As she neared the reef, a bullet hit her tank, the loud metal ping sounding like a death knell.

Bubbles erupted around her. She wouldn't have much time to hide before she ran out of air, and the bubbles would help them center on their target.

Her.

Then again, if they focused on the bubbles, she might be able to slip away.

Within a couple of yards of the reef, Kimo released the clips on her BCD, took a long last breath, spit the regulator from her mouth and let the BCD and tank sink to the ocean floor.

She swam for the reef, ducked into the maze of rocks and coral, releasing only a small stream of air from her lungs a little at a time. The bullets stopped streaming past her, but she could hear the fading pops. Once in the middle of the rocky outcroppings, she found a place where the rocks cleared the surface. Her lungs screaming for air, she surfaced long enough to take a breath, clear her snorkel and fit the mouthpiece between her teeth.

With her mask half in the water, she peered around the rocks, at the waves gently splashing, and watched as the men on the boat shined their spotlight down at the bubbles still rising from the ruined scuba tank.

A man's voice rose above the low rumble of the idling engine. "Can't see much around the bubbles."

"I know I hit him," another man said.

"You better hope he's dead."

"What about the girl?" a voice said. "Should I throw her in and let the fish finish her off?"

Kimo's breath caught and held. They had Alana.

"No. We can't risk her body washing ashore."

Her body.

Kimo fought the sob rising up her throat. Her friend… Was she dead?

"He's gotta be dead; the bubbles are slowing."

"We don't have time to dick around. We need to clean up the mess and get the hell out of here."

As the engine revved, the spotlight moved from where the tank had landed to sweep across the ocean's surface.

When it came her direction, Kimo ducked behind the rock and sank beneath the water, her snorkel the only part of her sticking up.

The light moved past her as the boat slowly circled.

Each time the boat and spotlight turned away, Kimo swam in the opposite direction, putting as much distance as she could between them. She stayed hidden in the reef, less afraid of sharks or stinging creatures than she was of the men with guns still searching the water for her.

All she had to do was wait for them to leave, then she could swim back to the dive boat and call for help.

Finally, the boat sped away.

Kimo watched as it slowed again, the spotlight slipping over the dive boat where they'd left it anchored.

Minutes later, the boat took off, with her dive boat in tow. So much for using the radio to alert the authorities. She'd have to go ashore and find a house to call for help. On the side of Maui where she was, homes were few and far between.

Once the two boats disappeared into the darkness, Kimo looked around at the blue of the bioluminescence, its brilliant glow undulating toward the shore, the tiny plankton sparking to life as the waves stirred them over the reef and against the sandy Shoreline.

While her best friend had been injured, and possibly killed, nature never even held its breath. The fish continued to swim, and stars twinkled overhead. Kimo struck out for shore. The sooner she could get a call through, the sooner the Coast Guard could be on the lookout for the boat and the men who'd taken Alana and bring her back.

CHAPTER 2

By the time Kimo made it to shore, she was cold and beyond exhausted. It took all her strength just to drag herself completely out of the water and up onto dry sand. She lay there, praying for the strength to keep going, knowing Alana's life depended on it.

For a moment, she closed her eyes.

Cool saltwater wrapped around her legs, tugging at her, chilling her body all over again.

She gasped and crawled further ashore.

The tide was coming in, creeping up the beach. She must have passed out. For how long?

Kimo's gaze shot to her dive watch. The last time she'd looked at the watch had been when she and Alana had climbed aboard the dive boat to refresh their scuba tanks and download photos on her computer. That had been...

Her stomach roiled. "Three and a half hours?" She

must have passed out. Her arms wobbled as she pushed herself up to a sitting position. Pain shot through her calf, where sand ground into a slash in her skin, made by the bullet that had struck her in her mad scramble to get away from the attackers.

Her head swam, and she swayed unsteadily. She couldn't pass out again. Too much time had passed already, and she was no nearer to getting help for Alana. She forced back the gray haze and stripped the flippers from her feet.

Fatigue and blood loss made it a struggle to get to her feet. She stood in her water shoes for several long moments, securing her balance as she scanned the nearby hillside. Most beaches on Maui had some way to access them. She just had to find it. This particular beach wasn't typical and didn't look like one of those highly visited strips of sand. Some beaches were only accessible by water. She hoped this one was not that case.

Having dived all around Maui, she tried to remember which beach this was on the west coast. They'd chosen to photograph the bioluminescence in a less-traveled area of Maalaea Bay. If she was right, this small beach was close to Kihei Road. It should have a gravel road or path leading up to the highway where she could wave down a car that might pass by in the wee hours of the morning.

Kimo slogged her way across the sand and through an outcropping of rocks to find a trail that led up the hill and emptied directly on the paved road. During the day, cars would park along the roadside. People would climb down to the beaches and snorkel.

In the middle of the night, the shoulders were empty. She prayed there would be some traffic on the road. If not, she'd work her way toward one of the resorts along the coastline. She looked left, then right. If memory served her correctly, left would take her to the nature preserve. Right would lead to one of the many resorts showcasing the Maui coast.

She turned right and plodded steadily, searching for headlights, porch lights, or brightly lit entrances to swanky resorts. At the first resort gate or any sign of other humans, she'd throw herself at the gate-keeper or the individual's mercy.

Kimo had gone a mile when a set of headlights appeared in the distance. Rather than stop and wait for it to come toward her, she staggered faster. The sooner she got help, the sooner they could find Alana.

As the headlights approached, Kimo raised her arms and waved frantically, standing in the center of the road, too tired to care if she got hit, yet praying the driver was paying attention and would see her before that happened.

At first, the vehicle didn't slow down. Kimo prepared to throw herself to the side at the last minute. Apparently, the driver finally spotted her and slammed on his brakes, bringing the vehicle to a skidding stop a few feet in front of Kimo.

Her heart raced, and her breathing was ragged. She reeled toward the driver's door. "Help me," she cried. "Please, help me."

The window lowered halfway, and a man peered out, a frown denting his forehead. "What's wrong?"

"My friend," Kimo said. "We were doing a night dive when we were attacked."

"By sharks?" the man asked, his eyes widening.

"No." Kimo shook her head. "By men. Do you have a cell phone?"

The man shifted into park and pulled out a cell phone. "I'm calling 911." He placed the call and pressed the phone to his ear. "I need to report an incident. A woman stopped me in the middle of the road, claiming to have been attacked on a night dive. Here, talk to her. She'll give you the details." He handed the phone to Kimo.

Her hand shaking as badly as her knees, Kimo pressed the device to her ear. "This is Kimo Kekoa. I was on a night dive with my partner, Alana Neal, when another boat attacked us. The boat struck my partner. The men on board dragged Alana up onto their boat. She was limp. I don't know if she was just injured or...dead." She swallowed hard on a sob and forced herself to continue.

"Are you sure it wasn't an accident?" the

dispatcher asked. "Maybe they were bringing her aboard to take her to a hospital?"

Kimo's jaw hardened. "It wasn't an accident. They shined a spotlight on her, aimed the boat directly at my friend and ran her over. Then they came back around and dragged her on board. I heard one of the men say, 'There has to be another diver. Find him. We can't leave loose ends.' Then they came after me, tried to run me over with their boat and then tried to shoot me in the water. Does that sound like an accident?" she asked, her voice hardening.

"No, ma'am."

"Either way, you need to send someone out here. Police, Coast Guard, National Guard—I don't care who. You need to find my friend."

The dispatcher's voice sounded in her ear, "We have your location based on the GPS coordinates of the cell phone you're speaking from. A police unit is on the way, and I've notified the Coast Guard. Help is on its way."

"Please, hurry," Kimo whispered. She handed the phone to the driver and sank to her knees in the middle of the road. Her body shook so hard her teeth rattled. She buried her face in her hands and sobbed.

A car door opened and closed. A moment later, a jacket was laid over her shoulders by gentle hands. "We should get you out of the middle of the road." The kind man who'd loaned her the cell phone closed his fingers around her arms and urged her to stand.

Her knees wobbling, Kimo let him guide her to her feet. He opened the back door of his car and eased her onto the back seat. "I hear sirens. Help is on its way," he assured her. While they waited, he pressed tissues to the wound on her calf in an attempt to stem the flow of blood.

Kimo sat in numb silence, her body still shaking, her vision blurred.

The distant wail of sirens grew louder. Before long, a Maui Police Department vehicle pulled up behind the man's car, and a uniformed officer got out.

He asked Kimo questions; she told him what she'd said to the dispatcher.

Within a few more minutes, an ambulance arrived.

An EMT rolled a stretcher toward her.

"I don't need an ambulance," Kimo said.

"Ma'am," the EMT said, "you've received a gunshot wound. A doctor should treat it."

"It's only a flesh wound," she argued as she fought a bout of nausea.

"Ma'am, blood loss and infection could lead to more serious complications," the EMT informed her. "A doctor needs to assess the damage and prescribe treatment that could include antibiotics or surgery."

Rather than keep her good Samaritan saddled with her, Kimo thanked him and let the EMTs load her on a stretcher.

As they strapped her down, she said, "I'm not the one who needs the medical attention," Kimo insisted. "My friend, Alana, is the one who needs the help." She glanced across at the police officer, tears welling in her eyes. "Please tell me they're looking for her."

The officer nodded. "Dispatch alerted the Coast Guard. They've sent out a helicopter from Oahu and a response boat from the Maui Coast Guard Station not far from here."

His words were welcome but not total relief. Until they found Alana alive, Kimo would be tied in knots, dreading the worst.

They loaded her into the waiting ambulance to transport her to Maui Memorial Medical Center in Wailuku on the other side of the island. On the way, she asked to use the EMT's cell phone.

He obliged and handed her his personal phone.

For a long moment, she stared at the numbers on the screen, her eyes blurring. "I don't know the number to dial," she admitted softly. "All my contacts are stored on my phone." She looked into the EMT's eyes. "My phone was on the dive boat." She held out the phone to the man.

He took it and asked. "Who are you trying to call?"

"My friend, Kalea." Her voice hitched on an errant sob. "Her husband, Hawk—Jace Hawkins—was a Navy SEAL. He runs a security agency on the Big Island."

The EMT's eyebrows rose. "The Brotherhood Protectors?"

Hope bloomed in Kimo's chest. "Yes. That's it. You know it?"

"I've heard of them. They've done some work on the island. I'm sure we can get a number for them. Maybe they you can hook you up with your friend's husband."

Kimo tried to sit up. The straps held her back. "Yes. Please. See if you can find it. The Brotherhood Protectors might be able to help us find Alana."

The EMT thumbed the information into his phone. A moment later, he grinned. "I have it. Calling now." He pressed his cell phone to his ear and waited. "This is Josh from the Maui EMS. I have Kimo Kekoa with me. She'd like to speak with Jace Hawkins. It is? Well, then let me hand her over." He held out the phone to Kimo.

Kimo's fingers curled around the cell phone as she pressed it to her ear. "Hawk?" Her voice shook.

"Kimo, what's going on?" Hawk's voice was gravelly, as if he'd just woken up. "Are you hurt?"

Hawk's deep voice filled Kimo's senses and made her eyes flood with tears. "They took Alana," she blurted out on a sob. With her thoughts in turmoil, the urgency of the situation forced her words out in a rush. "We were night diving. They ran her over, then dragged her aboard. They tried to run me over and fired bullets into the water... We have to find her. By now, they could be anywhere."

"Hey, hey," Hawk said in a calming tone. "Slow down and give me all the details. I have you on speaker. Kalea's here with me."

More tears welled in Kimo's eyes. "Oh, Kalea. I'm sorry to wake you both."

"Oh, Kimo. Don't worry about that. This is what we do. What's important is finding Alana."

"Kimo, I need you to start over," Hawk's voice cut in. "Who took Alana?"

"I don't know," she cried. "We were diving in Maalaea Bay. They showed up out of nowhere." She drew in a deep breath and let it out in an attempt to calm herself. Once she had her pulse and breathing under control, she started over, telling them everything she knew about the attack from the moment the boat showed up to when it disappeared with her dive boat in tow. "The Coast Guard has been alerted. They're sending out a boat from the Maui station and a helicopter from Oahu."

"About how long ago did this happen?" Hawk asked.

Kimo glanced at her dive watch. "Almost four hours ago." She swallowed hard on a sob threatening to rise up her throat. "We have to find Alana. She could've been hurt badly when the other boat struck her."

"We'll see what we can find out from the police

and Coast Guard. In the meantime, I'll send a couple of men out in boats to aid in the search and another to cover you."

"I'm not the one in trouble," Kimo insisted. "Send them all out to find Alana."

"They attacked you both," Hawk said.

"Why would they target us?" Kimo asked.

"You could've interrupted a nefarious assignation," Hawk said. "They might have been running drugs or illegal weapons. The fact that you spotted their boat could've been enough to make them want to eliminate any witnesses."

Kimo's breath caught as the fog clogging her mind cleared. She remembered what they'd found on the ocean floor. "The shipping container. Oh, my God." She pinched the bridge of her nose as the images of what they'd found roiled in her memory. "Right before we were attacked, we found a shipping container on the seabed."

"A shipping container?" Hawk prompted. "Did you see what was in it?"

"Yes. Oh, sweet Jesus... There was half a dozen decomposed bodies inside. I was so worried about Alana and getting away, I can't believe I forgot about those poor people."

"Did you tell the police?" Hawk asked.

"No." She looked at the EMT whose brow had furrowed. "I need to tell them. They need to know to send someone out there." Her chest squeezed so hard she could barely breathe. "If those men were responsible for the deaths of those people..." Tears slipped from the corners of her eyes. "They have Alana.'

"Talk to Kalea," Hawk said. "I'll relay the information to the Maui PD."

"Kimo," Kalea's voice sounded through the cell phone. "Alana's a strong woman. She's going to be okay. We have to believe that."

"If she's not already dead, they might just go to find a place to ditch her body," Kimo murmured. "Like they did those people in the shipping container. They were shackled to the walls. They had no way to escape."

"No wonder those men attacked you," Kalea said. "If they were responsible for that container being where you found it, and for the people inside, they wouldn't want any witnesses. Hawk's right to send one of his men to protect you."

"I saw men on the boat, but I wasn't close enough to identify any of their faces."

"Did you see a registration number on the side of the boat?" Kalea asked.

"No, and there wasn't a name across the back. I think it was one of those low-profile vessels. We heard it before we could see it. By then, it was too late."

"Yeah, but you saw what they'd done."

"Kimo," Hawk's voice came back on the line. "I'm on the phone with the Coast Guard about the shipping container. Did you happen to get the coordinates of the location?"

Kimo nodded and held up her dive watch. "I did. On my dive watch." She read off the coordinates to him.

Hawk repeated the coordinates to the Coast Guard representative and added, "Got it? Good." He paused. "Yes, I'll let you know if I learn of anything else. Thank you. Out here." Hawk said, "They're sending another boat to that location."

"Are you going to be all right?" Kalea asked. "I'd fly out tonight, but my plane is in the shop for annual maintenance."

"I'll be all right," Kimo responded without adding that Alana might not be okay. She had to believe she would be found. Alive. They couldn't give up on her.

"Kimo?" Kalea's voice sounded softly. "Are you still with us?"

Kimo stared up at the ceiling of the ambulance. "It was supposed to be a beautiful night dive to photograph marine life and the bioluminescence. And it was beautiful. I took some great shots. We found the shipping container but needed to surface to exchange tanks and find a pry bar to open the door of the container. I downloaded the photos onto my laptop."

She shook her head. "Now that laptop's gone with my boat."

"Did you take a photo of the shipping container before you came up for air?" Hawk asked.

Kimo frowned. "Just the outside of it. As I said, we needed leverage to get the door open wide enough to look inside. While Alana switched tanks, I downloaded the photos to my laptop and collected a pry bar."

"Kimo," Hawk's tone grew tense. "Was there any form of personal identification on the dive boat?"

"Yeah. My purse was on the boat with my cell phone, driver's license and boater education card inside."

"Which have your name and address on them," Kalea said.

"They'll know where to find you," Kelea said.

"And they have your laptop," Hawk said. "They have the photos you took. If they find out you didn't die, you're the only person who has seen the shipping container. Eliminate you, and the authorities have no proof."

"Unless the Coast Guard finds the shipping container," Kimo said.

"And if they don't find it?" Kalea said.

"The images are still on my camera." Kimo's gut clenched. She looked around the interior of the ambulance. "My camera!"

"Do you still have it?" Hawk asked.

"No. I must have dropped it when I released my BCD. I had pictures of the container and the victims on that camera." She fought against the restraints. "Let me out of here. Please."

The EMT laid a hand on her arm. "You need to see a doctor."

"I have to find my camera." She fumbled with the cell phone. It slipped from her fingers and clattered against the floor.

Kimo twisted and turned, clawing at the straps holding her on the stretcher. "Please, let me out."

The ambulance slowed and came to a halt.

"Okay, okay," the EMT said. "I'll let you out. But you might as well let a doctor see you. We're at the hospital." He released the straps around her legs first.

"I don't have time to see a damned doctor. I need to find my friend and my camera."

As soon as he released the strap around her chest, she sat up and launched herself toward the back door of the ambulance.

The EMT grabbed her arm. "Miss Kekoa, let me help—"

Still weak from exertion, Kimo fought to free herself from his grip. When her arm slipped free of his grasp, she was pulling so hard she flew in the opposite direction.

The back door opened at that moment.

Kimo fell through, crashing into a wall of hard muscle. The impact jarred what little air she had left in her lungs.

She would have dropped to the ground, except strong arms clamped around her and crushed her to the chest of the man they belonged to.

For a long moment, Kimo forgot how to breathe, and the automatic rhythm of her lungs was arrested as her heart stopped beating.

"Miss Kekoa, I presume?" a deep, warm voice sounded near her ear.

Kimo looked up into smoky gray eyes.

And blacked out.

CHAPTER 3

AFTER CONFIRMING the woman's identity with the EMT inside the ambulance, Rex Johnson carried Kimo into the Emergency Room. The EMT hurried ahead of him, clearing the path, opening "Authorized Personnel Only" doors and finding an empty gurney for Rex to deposit his charge onto.

Nurses and orderlies scurried around, securing an examination room for the patient and setting her up for an IV.

When they tried to shoo Rex out of the examination room, he refused to budge. "No way. I'm her bodyguard. I go where she goes."

A slim nurse sporting a tight ponytail stood toe to toe with him, her hands fisted on her hips. She was close enough that Rex could see her name on her badge. Nurse Bowman. "Bodyguard or not," she said, "at the very least have the decency to turn your back while we get her out of her wetsuit and under warm blankets to bring her body temperature up."

Rex stared down at the determined woman, his eyes narrowing. "I stay in the room."

"Fine," Nurse Bowman said in that way women did when they really didn't mean "fine." "About-face, soldier."

Rex reluctantly performed the maneuver, turning his back on the nurse and the woman he'd been sent to protect. He didn't bother to inform the nurse that he could monitor her every move reflected off the dark computer monitor perched beside him on a rolling cart. Though the image was a silhouette, he could see enough to tell whether they were helping or hurting his charge.

Nurse Bowman was joined by another carrying two pairs of trauma shears. Quickly and efficiently, they cut the wetsuit from the woman's body. They didn't stop at the wetsuit, continuing to remove the bright red bikini beneath. They dressed her in a hospital gown, without lifting her to tie it in the back.

Another nurse appeared, carrying an armful of warm blankets, covering the woman's body and tucking them around her.

He felt a stab of guilt for watching them strip and dress the woman, but having been awakened from a dead sleep, he was operating on limited information given in a quick briefing from his boss, Jace Hawkins.

Hawk had ordered him to the Maui hospital to protect Kimo Kekoa, who had been en route and would arrive minutes after him.

Hawk had said she'd been attacked. He wasn't sure by whom, or whether another attack was imminent. To do his job right, Rex couldn't take his eye off her until he had more data.

As it was, she'd practically flung herself out of the ambulance as if trying to escape. If he hadn't been there to catch her, she'd have crashed to the ground, compounding any injuries she'd already sustained.

He felt responsible for her, even above and beyond the fact he'd been assigned as her protector.

After they'd covered her, Nurse Bowman attached EKG patches, while another nurse set up an IV. They moved the monitor to a position beside the bed and connected the EKG leads.

The nurses whispered behind him.

He couldn't hear what they were saying and no longer had the monitor's reflection to see what they were doing. Rex turned to face them.

"Okay, we're done," the nurse with the dark ponytail said. "The doctor will be in momentarily."

The nurse who'd delivered the blankets scurried out of the room. The other two nurses didn't appear to be in a hurry to leave.

"Do you have any form of identification that would prove you're in fact this woman's bodyguard?" Nurse Bowman asked.

He pulled his wallet from his back pocket and removed one of the business cards Hawk had provided for each of the men working for the Hawaii branch of the Brotherhood Protectors. Along with the business card, he handed over his driver's license. "You can call my boss to verify and the Maui PD. They're aware of our work. They know we're legit."

A hospital security guard appeared in the doorway, his eyes narrowing on Rex. "Sir, if you're not a relative of this patient, you'll have to leave."

Rex straightened. "I'm Miss Kekoa's bodyguard. I've been assigned to protect her. I can't do that from the lobby."

"Until she regains consciousness and corroborates your claim, you'll have to leave." The security guard moved closer. "Hospital rules are in place to protect the patient."

Rex planted his feet slightly apart, prepared to defend his position. "I stay with my client."

"We can make this easy or do it the hard way," the guard said.

"He stays," a weak voice said from the hospital bed.

Rex turned to find Kimo Kekoa's dark hair fanned out across the white pillowcase, framing her pale face and dark, brown-black eyes, open to the drama happening in the examination room.

"You heard the lady," another voice said behind the security guard. A man wearing a white lab coat with a stethoscope tucked into a pocket entered the room. "Her bodyguard stays. Thank you, Officer Haoa. You were doing the right thing. Fortunately, our patient is able to speak for herself."

Officer Haoa nodded and left the room.

"Miss Kekoa, I'm Doctor Stanford. I understand you've had a rough night." The doctor pulled his stethoscope from his pocket and held it loosely in his hand. "Do you want your bodyguard to remain in the room while I conduct my examination, or would you prefer he step outside?"

Kimo's gaze met Rex's and held for a long moment. Finally, she sighed. "He can stay as long as he turns away during the exam."

The doctor cocked an eyebrow.

Rex turned away again, focusing on the sounds in the room while respecting his client's right to privacy. He took a moment to text Hawk.

Rex: With client. Doc with her now

Hawk: Good. Let me know if you need anything. Keep me in the loop

Rex: Roger

"She has a wound on her right calf," Nurse Bowman was saying.

"Ms. Kekoa, how did you acquire this wound?" the doctor asked.

"Someone shot me," she said, her voice soft, matter-of-fact.

"Gunshot wound. We'll clean it up and get you a

prescription for antibiotics. You don't want that site to get infected."

"Can we hurry this up?" she said, her tone tired but exasperated. "I'm not the one who needs medical attention."

"No?" the doctor queried.

"My friend," her voice caught. "She was with me. Now...who knows where they took her."

Rex turned to find tears in Kimo's eyes, her forearm resting on her forehead. "I need to get out of here and find her."

"That's why I'm here," a deep voice sounded from the doorway.

Rex stepped in front of the man attempting to enter. "Who the hell are you?"

The man held up an official-looking badge. "Detective Sykes," the man said. "I'm here to question Ms. Kekoa."

"Ms. Kekoa is being examined by the doctor," Rex said. "You can wait in the lobby until he completes his examination."

"And you are?" the detective demanded.

"Her bodyguard," Rex responded.

Detective Sykes snorted. "I understand Ms. Kekoa's dive partner is missing. The sooner I have answers to my questions, the sooner we can locate the missing woman."

"Let him in," Kimo said.

Rex's eyes narrowed at the detective. He held his

position a moment longer, then allowed the man to pass into the room.

Rex stayed close to the man. He might be a member of the Maui police force, but that didn't mean anything. In his experience, there were good cops and bad cops. Some people, no matter what their profession, could be bought. Rex wasn't going to trust anyone until he had all the information.

"Ms. Kekoa," the detective said, "where were you when your dive partner disappeared?"

"In Maalaea Bay on a night dive," she said.

"Had either of you been drinking?"

Kimo frowned. "Of course not."

"Were you under the influence of any drugs, prescription or otherwise?" the detective asked.

Kimo's frown deepened. "No. Absolutely not. I'm a professional diver. Drugs and alcohol have no place in the diving world."

"Not even for recreational use?"

"I said no. I don't drink and dive or do any manner of drugs." She shook her head from side to side. "My friend isn't missing because we were out partying in the bay. She was attacked. Run over and taken away by men in a boat."

"Are you sure your dive partner wasn't attacked by a shark? I understand that when you were brought into the ER, you were unconscious. Could you have had a lapse in memory?"

"No." Kimo tried to push up onto her elbows. Her

arms shook so much she collapsed back against the mattress. "I didn't have a lapse of memory. A boat ran her over. She was hit and hauled aboard the boat by men. They took her. She wasn't attacked by a shark. She was attacked by men."

"Are you sure it wasn't an accident. Maybe you two had an argument, didn't agree about something and she fell overboard? When she didn't come up, you got scared and manufactured this story about men in a boat attacking her and you. I mean, why would anyone attack a couple of divers in the middle of the night? It seems a bit far-fetched."

Anger that had been simmering inside Rex from the moment the detective had begun his interrogation flamed and grew. "Look, Detective, Ms. Kekoa told you what happened. Clearly, you're upsetting her with different scenarios that have nothing to do with what happened to her and her friend."

The detective held up a hand. "It's my responsibility to get to the truth. I'm simply doing my job."

"By badgering Ms. Kekoa with irrelevant questions?" Rex shook his head. "Try again."

"I suggest you back off, or I'll hit you with obstruction of justice."

"It's okay," Kimo said. "I'll answer his questions. Anything to get someone looking for Alana."

The detective met and held Rex's glare, then turned back to Kimo. "Were there any other witnesses to this attack?"

"The men who attacked us."

"No other people on the dive with you and your partner?"

"No." Kimo closed her eyes.

"So, it's only your word as to what happened out there?"

Her eyes opened to a slit as her brow descended. "Yes."

"Why did you wait so long to alert anyone about your missing partner?"

"Are you kidding me? Someone was shooting at me," Kimo exclaimed. "Then they took the dive boat with the radio. I had to hide in the reef until they left or risk being target practice. Then I swam a long way to shore. Trust me, I wanted to get back as soon as possible. That's my friend out there going through God knows what kind of hell."

The detective seemed unfazed by her story. "Could you be suffering from exposure, maybe enough that you could have hallucinated this entire scenario?"

Rex took a step forward.

Kimo held up a hand to stop him. "We were photographing the bioluminescence. It was a routine effort until we found a shipping container on the ocean floor. When we looked inside, there were decomposing bodies shackled to the walls. Maybe the men who attacked us had something to do with the dead people in the container. I don't know. All I do know is that they took Alana, my friend."

"You say you photographed the alleged shipping container." Detective Sykes lifted his chin. "Where are the photographs? Where's the proof?"

Kimo sighed. "I downloaded some of them to my laptop and the cloud. If I can borrow a laptop, I'll show you."

"What about the camera you were using?" Sykes asked. "Was it on the boat as well?"

Kimo shook her head. "Sadly, I lost it while fleeing the gunmen on the attacking boat. I must have dropped it when I released the BCD with the tank." Her brow dipped lower. "Are you going to do anything to find Alana?"

"We have people out there as we speak, looking for your dive partner." The detective squared his shoulders. "In the meantime, I suggest you don't leave the island. We might have more questions. Your dive partner, Alana Neal, might turn up. It hasn't even been twenty-four hours—hardly soon enough to file a missing person report."

"She's not just missing," Kimo's voice rose. "Alana was abducted. You can't wait twenty-four hours to search for her."

"We're handling it and looking for that missing dive boat as well. It's easier to hide a body than a boat."

Kimo's brow descended. "I don't give a damn about the boat. I want my friend back."

"That boat might have all the answers about your missing friend."

Rex didn't like the way the detective spoke to Kimo. It was as if he was implying Kimo was as responsible for the disappearance of the dive boat as she was for the disappearance of her friend.

"Are you accusing me of something, Detective Sykes?" Kimo asked, her voice rising.

The man held up his hands. "I'm not accusing you of anything. I'm just trying to get to the truth."

"I told you the truth," Kimo said.

"Well, then, you have nothing to worry about." He dipped his head. "Until we find Ms. Neal, don't leave the island." The man left the examination room.

Kimo stared after him, her brow furrowed. "He thinks I had something to do with Alana's disappearance and that I did something with the dive boat." She lay back against the pillow as the doctor and the nurse continued to work on the gunshot wound on her calf. "Has the whole world gone batshit crazy? Or have I?"

Rex's lips twitched. "Maybe a little of both…?"

Kimo snorted. "Thanks for the vote of confidence. Now, leave."

He cocked an eyebrow. "Like I told the security guard, I'm here until whoever is after you is caught."

"I don't need a bodyguard. I need to find my friend." She jerked her legs.

"You need to remain still until we complete our wound care," Nurse Bowman said.

"Sorry," Kimo said. "Trust me. I want you to finish so I can get out of here and start looking for Alana."

"Fortunately, the bullet missed any major arteries." The doctor straightened. "But infection is a possibility. I'll call in a prescription for antibiotics. Keep the wound clean and dry, take the medication, and it should heal within a couple of weeks. See your primary care physician for follow-up and stay away from men with guns."

Kimo's laugh choked on a sob. "That might not be an option, especially if they come after me again."

"That's why you have a bodyguard," the doctor said. "Hang onto him until you're in the clear."

The doctor lifted his chin toward Rex.

"On it," Rex promised.

After the doctor left the room, the nurse gave Kimo her discharge orders and asked what pharmacy she wanted the antibiotic sent to.

Kimo gave her the information and asked, "So, I can leave?"

Nurse Bowman nodded. "You need rest to recover from your ordeal."

"I need to find my friend. It's more likely her ordeal is worse than anything I've experienced."

The nurse nodded. "You can't help her if you pass out again."

"Can I take the hospital gown with me, seeing as I have no other clothes?"

The nurse's lips twisted. "Absolutely. Sorry about the wetsuit, but it's protocol to cut away restrictive clothing."

Kimo sighed. "I get it. Thanks for everything."

Nurse Bowman glanced toward the door. "Oh, good. Your wheelchair has arrived."

"I can walk out," Kimo insisted.

Nurse Bowman shook her head. "Hospital rules. You'll be escorted out in a wheelchair. I assume your bodyguard will take it from there."

Rex nodded. "I'll take it from there."

Kimo pressed her lips together. "Seeing as I don't have my car or street clothes, I'm at your mercy." She sat up and swung her legs over the side of the bed, exposing her bare backside to him.

Rex's lips quirked on the corners. "Do you want me to secure the gown in the back?"

"I do not," she said, reaching behind her neck to fumble with the ties.

"Here," Nurse Bowman hurried around the opposite side of the hospital bed and tied the strap at her neck and halfway down her spine, pulling the edges together to cover her naked back. "Take it easy getting up. You might feel a little dizzy."

Rex came to stand beside her and offered his arm.

Kimo frowned at him and pushed off the bed. "I can handle this." As soon as her feet hit the floor, her knees buckled.

Rex's arm shot out, wrapped around her waist and pulled her body against his. "Just go with it," he murmured. "Handle things later."

She didn't fight him—she couldn't at first.

The orderly brought the wheelchair close enough that all she had to do was turn around and sink onto the seat. A scowl marred her pretty face.

"I don't like being weak."

"You've had a bad day," Rex reminded her. "I'm sure you'll be back wrangling sea turtles and octopuses after a little sleep."

"He's right," the nurse said. "Rest."

Rex almost chuckled at the mutinous frown pulling her eyebrows into a V.

The orderly turned the wheelchair and rolled it out into the hallway and to the exit. "I'll wait with her while you bring your vehicle around."

Rex frowned. "I don't want to leave her."

The orderly shot a glance over his shoulder and then nodded. "Look, I'm not supposed roll patients out into the parking lot."

"That's okay," Rex said. "I'll take her from here."

"I can't let you take the wheelchair—" the orderly started.

"I won't need it." Rex bent and scooped Kimo up in his arms. The back of her hospital gown did little to cover her nakedness. The warm skin of her legs and back seared the nerves of his arms as he carried her out into the parking lot.

"Hey," she said, tugging the gown over her thighs, her cheeks flushing a pretty pink. "I can walk."

"Could you not argue for one minute?" he said. "It's faster this way."

Her lips formed a tight line, and her brow wrinkled. "Are you always so bossy?"

"Only when I need to be." He came to a stop beside a shiny black pickup. As he neared it, the doors automatically unlocked. Swinging her legs around, he reached for the doorhandle, pulled it open and unceremoniously deposited her into the passenger seat.

After closing her door, he hurried around to the driver's side and slid behind the wheel. "Where to?"

"I need clothes," she said. "My place." She gave him directions. Thankfully, her cottage was on the same side of the island as the hospital. They were there in less than fifteen minutes, as the pre-sunrise turned the night into a gray precursor to brilliant sunshine.

Before Rex could come around to her side of the truck, Kimo pushed open her door and slid out. Rex cursed beneath his breath and reached for her as her knees buckled. He caught her around her waist and steadied her. "Stubborn woman."

"Bossy man," she countered. "I can walk."

"Save it for when you have real clothes and shoes." Once again, he swept her up into his arms and carried her toward the little house.

"Shoot. My keys were in my purse on the boat the attackers took."

He climbed the steps and stiffened. "I don't think you'll need the keys."

"Why?"

Rex's arms tightened around her. "The door's open."

CHAPTER 4

REX PERFORMED an immediate about-face and hurried back to the truck.

"Where are you going?" Kimo squirmed in an attempt to get her feet on the ground.

"I need to get you somewhere safe."

"But someone broke into my house."

Rex nodded. "And might still be inside." He dumped her into the passenger seat and started to close the door.

Kimo's hand shot out to stop the door in mid-swing. "I'm not going anywhere. That's my house. I need clothes and need to know what's been taken. I have some expensive camera equipment inside worth a lot of money."

"Is your equipment worth more than your life?" he asked, his gaze narrowing on the house.

"Yes," she answered too fast and came back with, "No. But it's my house."

Rex dug his cell phone out of his pocket. "Then call 911 and report the break-in."

She didn't take the device. "What if it's not a break-in. What if I left the door unlocked, and it swung open? At least let me check it out before I involve the police."

His gaze narrowed at her cottage. "If you stay here and stay down, I'll clear the building. Only then can I allow you to go inside."

Kimo bristled. "There you go again, being all bossy."

His intense gaze met hers. "I can't protect you if you don't do what I tell you. As a former Delta Force operative, I'm trained and experienced in the art of clearing a building. Let me do my job, and I'll let you into your house."

Rather than fight a losing battle and delay entering her own home to assess the damage, Kimo nodded. "Deal."

He laid the phone in her palm. "If I'm not back out in two minutes, make that call to 911."

She nodded, her fingers curling around the cell phone. "But you'll be back, won't you?"

His lips curled up on one side. "I will. But hold onto that, just in case."

Then he leaned over her, opened the glove compartment and extracted a handgun.

Kimo's pulse fluttered. The shit was getting real when her bodyguard armed himself. "You always carry one of those?"

"When needed." He released the magazine, checked the bullets inside and slammed it back into the handle of the weapon. "Close and lock the door. I'll be right back."

"Hopefully," she murmured beneath her breath as she did as he'd said and closed and locked the door.

Rex tapped the glass. "Duck down."

Kimo slumped in her seat until she could barely see over the dashboard.

Rex hesitated for a moment and then hurried toward her house, the gun at the ready.

Again, he climbed the porch steps, approaching the door from the side, providing no clear target for anyone who might be inside.

Kimo's eyes rounded and her breath caught in her throat as Rex eased the door wider, then dove inside.

For what felt like an eternity, he remained inside.

Kimo strained her ears, listening for the sound of gunfire.

Just when she lifted the cell phone to punch in the three numbers, Rex, with his broad shoulders and imposing stature, stepped through the front door. He'd shoved the gun into his belt.

Kimo let go of the breath she'd held and sat up straighter. She couldn't lie to herself. She was remarkably glad to see him again.

As the former Delta Force operative descended the steps, Kimo unlocked her door and pushed it open. She waited for him to help her down.

"All clear." Rex reached into the truck and lifted her into his arms. When she opened her mouth to protest, he beat her to it with, "Just until we get you into some shoes. It's not safe to walk in there barefoot."

She frowned as he tucked his cell phone into his front shirt pocket and draped her arm around his neck. "So, it was breaking and entering?"

He nodded. "Emphasis on breaking."

Her heart sank, but she put it in perspective. "They're just things," she said. "I don't care about them. I care about Alana."

He nodded. "Hold that thought."

Rex carried her up the steps and into the house. "Where do you keep your shoes?"

"In the closet in my bedroom." As her gaze swept through the little house, her chest tightened. Furniture had been knocked over, the cushions on her couch slashed, knick-knacks and photo frames lay in splintered pieces and shattered shards around the room.

Rex strode with her down the hallway to the last door at the end of the hallway. When he stepped through, Kimo gasped.

The bedframe had been broken, and her mattress

slashed down the middle. The dresser she'd purchased at a flea market and refinished lay in pieces on its side, all the drawers removed, dumped and broken. "Why would someone destroy my things?" she whispered. "They aren't worth anything to anyone but me."

"Could they have been looking for something?"

"I don't own anything important but my cameras." Her eyes widened. "My cameras."

"Where do you keep them?"

"In the spare bedroom on the right side of the hall."

Rex shook his head. "I didn't see any cameras in that room or the one across from it. Did you keep them in a special storage place?"

Kimo shook her head. "No. I mostly leave them on a shelf in the closet. Did you look there?"

Rex nodded. "I looked there, under the bed and in the chest of drawers."

"They took my cameras," she said, her eyes welling. "They're the tools of my trade. Without them, I can't do my job."

"Did you have them insured?"

She nodded. "But it takes time to replace them. Many were special orders." Kimo sighed. "Again. Not as important as finding Alana."

"Things can be replaced."

"People can't," she concluded. "There's no broken glass in here. You can set me on my feet."

He glanced around before lowering her feet to the ground. His arm remained around her back.

She'd never admit to him that she found his touch reassuring. Though she appreciated his presence at the moment, he wouldn't be around forever. She might as well regain her balance and stand on her own two feet.

Kimo stepped away from him, clutching the back of her hospital gown to keep from mooning the man.

His hand fell to his side.

The loss of his gentle support almost made her lose her balance again.

She squared her shoulders and bent to retrieve a pair of running shoes from her closet. She had to dig for them as all her hanging clothing had been stripped from the rod, ripped and dropped amongst the shoes.

Her beautifully organized and clean home had been reduced to a nightmare of disruption so overwhelming that tears welled in her eyes. She angrily tossed aside a blouse that had been torn down the middle of the back.

"Are you okay?" Rex asked.

"Of course, I'm not okay," she cried. "I can't find my stupid running shoes."

"What color?"

Her thoughts were so disjointed that she had to think hard to remember. "Sea-foam green."

Rex dropped to his haunches beside her and dug

into the clothing. He found one of her shoes and handed it to her. A few seconds later, he located the other.

Then he held up one unscathed shirt after another until Kimo agreed on a cream-colored short-sleeved pullover. She pointed at a pair of faded blue jeans that had also escaped destruction.

He helped her back to her feet. "Need help dressing?"

Her cheeks heated. "No. I think I can do that on my own."

"I'll wait in the hallway. Call out if you feel dizzy or light-headed."

"I'll be okay," she said. "Go."

Rex stepped out into the hallway.

Once he was out of sight, Kimo dug through the pile of panties and bras and selected those that had survived the intruders.

She dragged on panties and the jeans, then pulled the gown over her head and tossed it into the dirty clothes basket in the corner of her room. She could have just left it on the floor and collected it with the other items whenever she felt like cleaning again.

That wouldn't be anytime soon.

As she hooked the bra in place, she called out, "Did you notice if my desktop computer survived?"

"Where was it?"

"It was in the same room as my cameras."

"I'm looking in that room now," he said. "No

cameras and no desktop computer. There are cords still plugged into the wall."

"Damn," she murmured. "I need a computer so that I can access my cloud storage. The photos I uploaded might tell us more about the shipping container, like who it belongs to and when it was lost at sea."

"We could visit a library. They usually have computers available to the public. Or if you trust me, I can take you to my apartment. I have a laptop there. Do you want me to call the police now to report the break-in?"

She pulled the shirt over her head and down her torso. "Yes, now that we know for certain."

"On it," he said. "Try not to touch too much. They might lift prints off surfaces."

After she found socks, she sat on the mattress and pulled them on, then her shoes. She tied the laces and pushed to her feet, feeling less like an invalid and closer to herself. Yes, a little weak, and the gunshot wound stung on her calf, but she was functional and ready to take on the task of finding Alana.

Sunlight filled her living room through the big picture windows that looked out over her small backyard with its paving stones meandering through her garden of blossoming bougainvillea, hibiscus and plumeria trees.

After years of building her photography business, she was finally successful and had saved enough money to put a down payment on a house of her own. On most days, the view calmed her and made her happy she'd chosen this house.

Today, all she could think about was Alana. Was she alive? Where had the men taken her?

Rex emerged from the hallway, tucking his cell phone into his pocket. "The Maui PD is sending a unit."

"I guess that means we have to wait to go to the library." She shuffled around the room, bending over to pick something up and stopping before she could. "It's hard to resist the urge to clean." She raised her hands. "I know. I can't compromise any fingerprints they might find." Rather than reach for items, she wrapped her arms around herself and waited for the police to arrive.

"How long have you lived in this house?" Rex asked.

"Two and a half years," she said, turning slowly, taking in the destruction. "I was so happy to move into my own home." She shrugged. "Well, my name's on it, even though the bank owns more of it than I do." She faced him. "What about you? You say you live in an apartment. Have you ever owned a house?"

He nodded. "I own a few."

Her brow furrowed. "Do you own your apartment?"

Rex shook his head. "I rent it."

"Why do you rent if you own a few homes?"

He shrugged. "They're part of my investment portfolio. I rent them out. It's supposed to be passive income. Though I spend time doing the maintenance on them."

"Investments, passive income... Why do you work with the Brotherhood Protectors? Sounds like you don't need to."

"I like to keep busy and to use the skills I learned in the Army. Can't always do that, managing property."

"Did you learn about investments and purchasing property in college?"

He shook his head. "Not so much in college; I learned at home. My father drilled it into me. He tried to teach me all there was to know about business and finances from the moment I learned to read."

"Did he want you to grow up able to take care of your family?"

"No," Rex said, his lips thinning. "He wanted me to take over the family business after he retired."

"Was that a bad thing?" she asked.

He snorted. "While other fathers taught their sons how to throw a football, mine taught me how to invest in stock markets and how to leverage mortgages to build a portfolio of assets."

"I take it you would rather have been out throwing a football."

"Actually, I drank it in, hoping that by showing

interest in what he did, he would take an interest in me."

"Did he?"

He shrugged. "Only as far as what I could add to his company. When I went to college, he chose my degree. When I told him I'd switched my degree field to history and political science, he cut my funding, saying he wouldn't pay for a useless degree. When I was ready to be serious about my studies, we could talk."

"What did you do?"

His lips curved upward. "I joined the Army, worked hard and earned my way into Delta Force."

"Was your father proud of you then?"

He laughed. "No. He cut all ties with me when I joined the Army."

Kimo's heart pinched hard in her chest. "What about your mother?"

"She died when I was at the end of my sophomore year of college. My mother was the only person in my father's house who made living there tolerable. She made me promise to live my life the way I wanted, not to let anyone take my choices away."

"Thus, the change in your course of studies," Kimo said softly.

Rex nodded.

"Any regrets about your decision to join the Army?" Kimo asked.

"None," Rex said. "My father disowned me. My

only family, my mother, was gone. In the Army, I found myself and my brothers in arms. I learned that love and loyalty weren't determined by the blood in your veins, but by the blood you were willing to spill for people you care about." He glanced out the front window. "Looks like the Maui PD is here." A frown brought his brow low. "Great, it's Detective Sykes."

Kimo shook her head. "Did it have to be him?"

The detective left his vehicle and climbed the steps to Kimo's cottage.

"I'll get the door," Rex said.

"Thanks," Kimo said and remained in the middle of the living room. The further away from the odious detective, the better.

Rex opened the door before the man could knock. "Can I help you?"

"I'm here to speak to Ms. Kekoa." The detective glanced past Rex to where Kimo stood. "She called in a disturbance?"

"I called in about a break-in at her home. Are you here to dust for prints?"

The detective's brow descended. "I'm here to help. Perhaps I could speak with Ms. Kekoa, as this is her home."

Rex remained fully blocking the doorway, his arms crossing over his chest. "Are they sending someone who could actually help document the crime without interrogating the victim?"

"It's okay, Rex," Kimo said. "I'll talk to the detective."

For another long moment, Rex remained in the doorway. Finally, he took a step back, leaving barely enough space for the man to squeeze by.

His frown affixed to his face, Detective Sykes eased past Rex and studied the room. "Was your home in this condition when you left it...was it yesterday?"

Kimo fought the urge to roll her eyes but didn't fight the sarcasm shooting past her vocal cords. "Of course. I'm in the process of redecorating. I'm going for a post-ransacked feel." She shook her head. "No, this is not how it looked when I left yesterday afternoon."

"Are there any items missing?" he asked.

"My cameras and computer," she said.

"Were there images or data on any of your equipment that could possibly inspire someone to steal the items?"

"Shouldn't you be asking if the equipment was expensive? The items were expensive when I first purchased them. As used electronics, they don't hold much value to anyone but me. They're my livelihood. Without them, I can't operate my photography business. Replacing the items will take time and a lot more money."

"You said you could tap into the cloud for the

images you downloaded from your dive last night. Were you able to do that?"

"Considering I just got home from the hospital only to find my home a shambles and my computer and cameras missing...tapping into the cloud would be a no."

The detective frowned. "I have a laptop in my cruiser. Perhaps you could use it to tap into your data."

Kimo's brow twisted. "I suppose I could." She wasn't fond of the detective or his interviewing techniques.

"I'll be right back. And, yes, there's a unit on its way to process this crime scene."

After Sykes left the house, Rex met and held Kimo's gaze. "You okay?"

She nodded. "Still a little weak, but I'm holding my own."

Rex's gaze swept over her face. "You say the word when you've had enough, and I'll escort the detective out."

It was nice to have someone worry about her for once. It had been a long time since her parents died. Not that she thought of Rex as a substitute for her parents—not with his rugged good looks, broad shoulders and the strength to carry her around like she was as light as a feather.

Talk about sweeping a girl off her feet... Her pulse

skittered through her veins, her body heating all over again, especially at her core.

Moments later, Detective Sykes was back with a laptop sporting a hardened case. He flipped it open and turned it toward her.

Kimo didn't like logging into a strange computer with her username and passwords, but that's what it would be like if she went to a library. Surely, it would be more secure on a police detective's device.

She quickly logged onto her cloud storage and waited for all the files to appear.

And waited...

Nothing came up. No files. No photos. No documents.

"What the—" She logged off and started over, keying in her username and password.

Again, the screen remained empty of the files she'd so meticulously organized with all the photos she'd taken for the past ten years.

"This can't be right," she said, her heart in her throat. "Something must be wrong with my storage provider."

"Why do you say that?" Rex came to stand behind her, looking over her shoulder at the empty screen.

"My files. My photos. They're not here. Everything's gone." She looked up a phone number for the data storage company and held out her hand toward Rex. "May I borrow your cell phone?"

He laid it in her palm. "What are you going to do?"

"I'm going to call and see if they're having technical difficulties that could keep me from accessing my data." She entered the numbers and placed the call.

Five minutes later, after working with their technical support, she ended the call and stared at the empty screen, her heart sinking to the pit of her belly. "It's gone. Ten years of work..."

Gone.

Rex laid his hands on her shoulders and pulled her back gently until she leaned into him.

"Are you certain you entered your username and password correctly?" the detective asked.

"Yes," Kimo said. "I logged in twice, and the tech support person verified. The files are gone."

"Does that mean the photos you took yesterday are gone as well?" the detective asked.

She nodded, stunned and heartsick. "Everything. My laptop stored a lot of the images, and my desktop had copies of everything except what I took last night."

"And both computers are gone," Rex said.

The detective grunted. "I guess you don't have the proof we need that there was a shipping container filled with dead people."

"But they were there," she insisted.

"If they really are, the Coast Guard should find

them. If not... I'm sorry. With no bodies, no photos and no other witnesses, it's hard to dedicate resources to investigate it."

Kimo frowned at the detective. "And Alana? A *live* woman I *witnessed* being abducted. Are you going to shelve that investigation as well?"

"We're looking into it." The detective reached for the laptop. "Again, until we know more, don't leave Maui."

"And where would I go?" She raised her hands, palms up. "This is my home."

"We'll be in touch," the detective said and left the house.

Kimo shook her head from side to side, trying and failing to absorb it all. "My life's work has been wiped clean, along with the digital proof that there were dead people chained to a shipping container at the bottom of Maalaea Bay. The equipment I used in my business is gone. I'll have to postpone the work I had scheduled, lose contracts and disappoint customers. Worst of all, my friend is missing. What now?"

"I don't know, but that detective doesn't appear to be in a hurry to find your friend or that shipping container." Rex ran his hand over the stubble on his chin, his eyes narrowing thoughtfully. Then he nodded as if agreeing with himself. "I have an idea."

"Good," Kimo said, "because all I'm coming up with is doing the job ourselves. If we can't get the

Maui PD working on finding Alana, we can't just sit around and wait."

Rex nodded. "That was where my idea was heading." He paced across the floor. "We have access to a computer guru who makes hackers look like amateurs. I'll contact him and see if he can find backups of your online storage, including the images you uploaded before the attackers stole the boat."

Kimo's eyes widened. "He can do that?"

Rex shrugged. "I can't guarantee anything, but if it can be done, he's our man."

"If he can get the images I took of the shipping container, there might be some form of identification on it."

Rex nodded. "We might be able to track its origin." Rex's brow wrinkled. "You say you rented the boat?"

"I did, from Jako's Diving Adventures. I need to contact Jako and let him know about the boat."

"Let's check with him and see if the boat has turned up or if he had a tracker on it," Rex suggested. "Do you have his number?"

"I'd rather give him the news in person," Kimo said.

"Are you sure you're up to it?" Rex asked.

Kimo drew in a deep breath and let it out. "I have to be."

"And I'll check with my boss. He sent some of the

team we have on Maui to search the waters around Maalaea Bay. I'd like to know if they found anything."

Kimo glanced out the front window as a Maui PD cruiser rolled into her driveway. "Did the detective forget something?"

Rex came to stand beside her as a uniformed policeman stepped out of the vehicle.

Kimo's lips pressed together. "Maybe Sykes sent him to actually investigate the break-in."

"Let's hope he knows what he's doing," Rex said. "I'm not convinced Sykes does."

"I hope he makes it fast. I feel like the longer we wait to search for Alana," Kimo swallowed hard before continuing, "the less chance we have of finding her."

CHAPTER 5

THE MAUI PD officer got started dusting a million surfaces in the cottage for prints.

Rex hooked Kimo's arm and guided her out onto the front porch. He sat on the porch steps and motioned for Kimo to join him.

She sank beside him and stared out at the police vehicle while Rex pulled out his cell phone.

The first call was to his boss. He clicked on the number and put it on speaker so that Kimo could hear the conversation.

"Rex," Hawk answered, "tell me what's happening."

"I have Ms. Kekoa with me. You're on speaker."

"Kimo," Hawk said. "How are you feeling?"

"Alive. Not yet one-hundred percent, but getting there," Kimo said. "Rex will fill you in."

Rex took over and filled Hawk in on what had

occurred since he'd texted his boss that he'd arrived at the hospital and found Kimo.

"I'm glad you're with her," Hawk said. "Kalea was worried about her and Alana."

"Have you heard from the guys you sent out on the water?" Rex asked.

"I just got word from them," Hawk said. "I'm sorry to say they didn't find Alana or the missing boat. I touched base with my contact at the Coast Guard headquarters on Oahu. They'd sent out a helicopter, but they haven't had any more luck either."

"What about the shipping container?" Kimo asked. "Did the Coast Guard find it?"

"I talked to my Maui contact half an hour ago. They went to the coordinates you gave us." Hawk paused. "They didn't find a container or bodies."

Kimo's face paled.

"Are you sure of the coordinates you gave us?" Hawk asked.

"I used them to relocate the box on our second dive. They were accurate," Kimo said. "They didn't find the container?"

"No," Hawk reconfirmed.

"How can that be possible?" Kimo shook her head, her brow creasing. "It was there. Alana and I saw it. We pried it open to look inside. The bodies..." Her voice trailed off. "It was surreal, like a scene from a horror film."

"Is it possible for a twenty-foot shipping

container to be dragged up from the ocean floor in the amount of time it took for Kimo to get to help?" Rex asked.

"Since it was almost four hours from the time of the attack to when she notified the police, there's a chance someone could've located and removed the container. But it would have to be someone with specialized equipment and a boat or ship large enough to handle it."

"I should've gotten help sooner," Kimo said. "I took too long."

"It's not your fault you were attacked." Rex slipped an arm around her and gently pulled her close. The woman had been through a lot. "And it's not your fault they took your friend."

"But I should've done more." Her body trembled against Rex.

"You did the best thing by getting away from them and letting people know what happened," Hawk assured her.

"Hawk, could we pull Swede in on this conversation?" Rex turned to Kimo. "Swede's the tech guy I told you about."

"On it," Hawk said.

A moment later, another voice joined the call.

"Swede here. Hawk gave me the digest version of what's going on. What can we do to help?"

"Is it possible to reclaim files that have been wiped clean from an online storage site?" Rex asked.

"It's possible, but it depends. Does the online storage site have automated backups? If so, how often do they perform the backups? Did you save a copy on your desktop? If so, does your desktop or laptop have another data backup system protecting your data?"

Kimo pinched the bridge of her nose. "I don't know the answers. All I know is that when I logged into my online storage service, my files were gone."

"Text me the name of your service and your username and password," Swede said. "I'll see what I can find."

"If you manage to get to that data," Rex said, "look for the images she uploaded last night. There should be one of the shipping container, sitting on the ocean floor. Look for any identifying marks on it that might lead us to its origin."

"Will do," Swede said. "If there's anything else you need, don't hesitate to ask. We're here to help."

Kimo's lips tipped upward a little. "Thanks."

Rex gave her a quick, encouraging nod. "We're going to the dive shop that rented the boat to Kimo to see if they had a GPS tracker on it."

"Hopefully, they did," Hawk said. "Makes sense to have them on rentals."

"Let me know if I need to check into the rental company's tracking database," Swede said.

"We will," Rex assured the man.

"In the meantime, I'll see what I can find of Ms.

Kekoa's online files and the picture she took of the shipping container."

"The break-in at Kimo's house could've been by a thief looking for expensive equipment to pawn," Hawk said. "But given the fact her online storage was wiped, and her computer and photography equipment were taken so soon after she spotted a sunken shipping container with human remains, I'd lean toward this being more than a random theft."

"Agreed," Rex said.

"Someone doesn't want Kimo's photos to get out," Swede said. "Got it. I'll start digging now and get back with you as soon as I can."

"Thanks, Swede," Rex said.

"Out here," Swede said.

"Rex, you still on the line?" Hawk asked.

"Still here," Rex responded

"Any chance you and Kimo can find the camera she dropped when she was evading the attackers?"

Rex cocked an eyebrow in Kimo's direction.

Kimo drew in a deep breath and let it out slowly. "I don't know. I have the coordinates for where the shipping container was. After the attack, I was more concerned about dodging bullets than saving more sets of coordinates." She frowned. "They shot a hole into my tank, and I released the BCD to buy time for me to get away, hoping they would follow the bubbles from the air escaping through the bullet hole. I'm almost sure I dropped the camera when I released my BCD."

"But that's a big bay," Rex said.

"Yeah," Kimo said. "But that camera and the images on it might be the only connection we have to that shipping container and the people responsible for the deaths of those chained inside."

"That container might be our only lead as to who took Alana," Rex said. "Whoever dropped it into the ocean obviously didn't want anyone else to find it. The men who attacked you could've been the ones sent to locate and retrieve the container."

Kimo shook her head. "Locate and guard, maybe. Their boat wasn't big enough or equipped with the means to extract a container that size from the ocean floor—especially so quickly."

"Like you said, they could've been the scouting and protection crew there to keep others from discovering their ugly secret," Hawk said. "Which means, they'll want everything to do with your find erased."

Kimo shivered. "Including my laptop, home computer, online storage and the camera I lost when I fled."

"And you," Rex added softly.

"Exactly," Hawk said. "Stay close to her."

Rex glanced toward his pretty client. "That's the plan."

After Hank ended the call, Kimo looked up into Rex's eyes. "We need a boat."

"Do you think you can find the camera?"

Her jaw hardened. "I have to find the camera. Alana's life might depend on it. When we meet with Jako, I'll ask if he has another boat I can rent."

Rex and Kimo went back into the house to find that the officer had finished gathering evidence in the living room and had moved on to the bedrooms.

Rex insisted that Kimo sit in one of the chairs he picked up off the floor. She looked like she was about to fall over. No sleep, a gunshot wound plus a strenuous swim to get from where they'd been diving to the shore had to have taken their toll on the woman.

She sat quietly observing the officer as he moved in and out of the bedrooms.

Rex was surprised she hadn't gotten up to start cleaning. Perhaps she was conserving her energy for when they paid a visit to Jako's Diving Adventures. If the man had a boat and dive gear for her to rent, they could be heading out on a dive in Maalaea Bay before noon.

Less than an hour after the Maui police officer arrived, he finished dusting for prints, photographing the damage and inking Rex's and Kimo's prints to rule them out when comparing them with the prints he'd found.

The man took their statements and wrapped up, leaving soon after.

Kimo walked through the house, the dark circles under her eyes more pronounced as she took in the destruction and the mess left behind from the powder the officer had used to lift latent prints.

"As much as it bothers me to see my home in this condition, I'm not going to start the cleanup process yet." Kimo turned to Rex. "However, I'd like to take a quick shower before we go to Jako's. I still have salt in my hair and on my skin, and it's chafing."

"What about your injury?"

Her lips twisted. "I'll have to keep that leg out of the shower."

"On the way over to Jako's, we need to stop by your pharmacy and pick up the antibiotics the doctor prescribed," Rex said.

Kimo grimaced. "I hate taking pills."

"You'd hate getting an infection more. How do you plan to keep that injury dry if we go looking for your camera?"

Kimo shrugged. "Tape and plastic wrap? I can pick up something at the pharmacy." Kimo gathered clothing from the floor of her bedroom and paused at the bathroom door. "Thanks for having my back. I'm not sure how I would've handled walking into my house the way it is by myself."

"I'm here to protect," he said. "It's what I do."

Her lips quirked. "And manage property and investments. What is it your father does for a living?"

Rex shifted his gaze away from Kimo, his body stiffening. "He owns his own corporation."

"What kind of corporation?" she asked.

His gaze came back to hers. "Get your shower."

CLUTCHING her clothing to her chest, Kimo ducked into the bathroom and closed the door behind her.

Her bodyguard was a bit touchy when it came to his father. Asking questions about the man hadn't earned her any points.

Kimo stripped out of her clothing, turned on the tub faucet and adjusted the temperature. When it was warm enough, she stepped over the rim of the tub, keeping her injured calf outside the shower curtain. Though it was an awkward stance, she managed to duck beneath the spray.

She quickly rubbed shampoo into her hair and over her body, washing away the crusty feeling of dried salt on her skin. All the while, her thoughts poured over the events of the previous night, finding the shipping container and its grisly contents, watching helplessly as Alana had been abducted and crashing into Rex's arms as she'd flung herself from the back of the ambulance.

So much had happened. The one thing in all of it that had kept her grounded was the tall, broad-shouldered former Delta Force soldier who'd come to protect her.

She'd learned to count on herself after her parents had died in a plane crash when she'd still been in college. An only child, she'd had no family to fall back on. Though her friends had helped her through her grief, Kimo prided herself on her independence. She normally refused help, preferring to manage situations under her own steam.

But she had to admit, this situation was different. The stakes were higher. Secrets were deadly, and people had died. Whoever was responsible was going to great lengths to keep those secrets. They obviously had the personnel, equipment and connections to make it happen.

As the only person raising a red flag that something horrible had happened, Kimo couldn't—no, wouldn't—stop striving for justice for Alana and the people who had drowned in the shipping container. Those responsible had erased the evidence; now all they had to do was remove the only other witness.

Her.

Though she'd been resistant at first to having a bodyguard, the gravity of her predicament was becoming clear. She needed someone to have her back, especially if she planned to go after the camera and start her own search for Alana.

It didn't hurt that her bodyguard was strong and attractive in that ruggedly sexy way.

If she weren't so worried about Alana, she would be tempted to explore that attraction.

Having lived on Maui all her life, Kimo knew most of the eligible men who called the island their home. She'd dated a few but hadn't felt anything that made her want anything more than friendship.

For too long, she'd been looking for that spark—the mind-blowing "ah-ha" moment her parents had told her they'd experienced with their first kiss.

She'd watched her friends fall in love and realized it was different for everyone.

Her friend Kalea had gone from enemies to lovers when her father had saddled her with Hawk as a secret bodyguard. She'd resented being shadowed until her shadow had saved her life. Theirs had been a fiery discovery of their love. Now, they couldn't imagine life without each other and their baby only made them happier. Hawk had settled with Kalea on the Big Island and set up a Brotherhood Protectors branch, recruiting former military to protect those who needed it.

Leilani, her beautiful friend she'd known since they were in grade school together, had found love with one of those men working for Hawk. She'd literally fallen into his arms while giving a guided tour. Their struggles through danger had brought them close, sparking a love so strong that Kimo could only imagine what that was like.

Then there was Kiana, a former model, now manager of a Maui resort. She'd fallen for one of

Hawk's men when he'd helped her find her missing sister on Oahu.

Kimo frowned. Was it her turn? Was she supposed to be like her friends and fall for her bodyguard?

She shook her head. Rex struck her as a man with intense focus on his mission. As well, now wasn't the time to consider dating anyone.

Alana had been abducted. People had drowned trapped in a shipping container and Kimo's home and life were under attack.

Who had time for such silliness as love?

She squared her shoulders, rinsed the soap from her hair and body and turned off the water, convinced her thoughts were on overdrive and out of control.

Like Rex, she needed to focus on finding that camera. To do that, she needed a boat and scuba gear.

After quickly drying herself, careful not to disturb the dressings on her leg, she pulled on a swimsuit and dragged jeans and a T-shirt over them.

Dressing was fast. Taming her long, wavy hair took twice as much time. She'd inherited her mother's Hawaiian genes with her thick black hair, dark eyes and short stature. Though having long hair was a hassle for scuba diving, she hadn't had the heart to cut it short. It reminded her of her mother every time she looked in the mirror.

Once she'd pulled the tangles out, she wove the

damp tresses into a single braid that hung down the middle of her back and secured it with a ponytail. Then she brushed her teeth, grimaced at her makeup-less reflection and shrugged. "What you see is what you get." Finding Alana was more important than makeup.

Kimo left the bathroom and went in search of Rex. He wasn't in the living room, but there was evidence he had been there. Overturned furniture had been set to rights and broken glass had been swept away. Even the black dust the officer had used to lift prints had been cleaned off most surfaces. In the kitchen, the drawers were back where they belonged, their contents either in the sink or loaded into the dishwasher.

And no Rex.

Noise from the laundry room captured her attention. She crossed through the kitchen and pushed the door open to the small room that served as the laundry room and pantry, where she stored her dry goods.

Rex was in the process of transferring a blanket from the washer to the dryer. When he straightened, he noticed her standing there. "I didn't think you'd mind if I straightened up."

"You know, you don't have to clean my house." Kimo shook her head. "I'll get to it eventually."

"I don't like standing around when there's work to be done." He tipped his chin toward the living room. "The pictures of turtles, coral and fish that were hung on the wall...did you take them?"

Kimo nodded. "I'm afraid they're too damaged to salvage. And if I can't recover my files, I won't be able to replace them."

"Give Swede time. He's really good with computers and the internet." He turned to the dryer, adjusted the settings and pressed the start button. When he faced her, his gaze swept her from head to toe. "Feel better after your shower?"

She nodded. "Almost normal, though it was a challenge to shower with one leg out of the tub. I don't know why I bothered to hang it out of the shower when I'll be diving again sometime today."

Rex frowned. "I thought you said you would tape something over it to keep it dry."

"I will. But it might not last in saltwater." She glanced up into his gray eyes, her earlier thoughts in the shower making her look at him in a different light.

No. He wasn't her type, she told herself. Too intense. Too serious.

Determined to shelve Rex as a potential love interest, Kimo forced a smile, relieved and a little embarrassed that her thoughts had taken that path. Thankfully, mind-reading wasn't a thing, or she'd really be embarrassed.

She wondered how many female clients he'd worked with and if any had imagined themselves in love with him. He did have incredibly broad shoulders and smoky gray eyes. His dark blond, almost brown hair had enough of a wave to make a girl want to run her fingers through it, especially when an errant strand fell over his forehead.

She lifted her hand.

"Ready?" he asked.

Kimo froze, realizing she'd almost reached out to smooth that strand of hair back in line with the rest.

She redirected her hand to tuck an imaginary hair behind her ear. Heat rose up her neck and into her cheeks. "Uh. Sorry. What did you say?" she asked, flustered at her near slipup.

"Are you ready?"

She blew out a breath in an attempt to calm herself and then nodded. "I am." *Ready to find Alana, not to touch Rex's hair.* "Let's go." *Before I do something stupid.*

She needed to be more like Rex and focus on the mission. Exhaustion was really taking its toll on her if she was fantasizing about a man she'd just met.

Rex was first to exit the house, where he paused to study the surroundings. Apparently satisfied she was safe, he stepped out of the doorway.

As Kimo walked by him, all her senses were on alert. So much so, she could smell the plumeria growing on the tree that shaded the porch and the cologne Rex wore.

Yeah, trauma and lack of sleep. That had to be it.

He held the door open to the passenger side of his truck and helped her up into the seat with a hand at the small of her back.

Once she'd settled, she fumbled with the seatbelt.

Rex stepped up onto the running board, reached across her and secured her belt. His shoulder grazed her breast, sending sparks of electricity shooting through her body.

He paused on his way back across her and stared into her eyes. "Are you all right?"

Again, her cheeks heated. "Why do you ask?"

"Your face is flushed." He reached out and touched his palm to her forehead. "You don't feel feverish, but our first stop will be the pharmacy for those antibiotics. I don't think it's a good idea for you to dive today."

"I'm fine," she insisted. "Really. Besides, I'm the only one available who saw that container and then escaped the gunmen. No one else could come close to figuring out where I might've dropped the camera. The chances of finding it out there are pretty slim— impossible without me."

Rex touched the bandage on her calf, shaking his head. "I just don't think it's a good idea."

"We don't have much of a choice. No one else is having any luck locating Alana. She's my friend. I have to do something. She'd do the same for me."

Rex nodded. "Let's get those antibiotics and pay a

visit to the dive shop. Maybe by the time we get to Jako's, Swede will have recovered your data."

"Hopefully, the image of the container will show something useful marked on it to lead us to who owns it."

"Then we'll follow that trail." He dropped to the ground, strode around the hood and slid in behind the wheel. "In the meantime, we'll play the diving by ear."

Kimo didn't argue. It served no purpose. If she needed to dive, she'd do it.

CHAPTER 6

REX STOPPED at the pharmacy and went inside with Kimo to collect the antibiotics the doctor had ordered. He paid for the medicine and brushed aside her assurances that she would pay him back.

While they were there, they picked up waterproof dressings in case their only choice was to go after the camera.

He wasn't convinced Kimo was up to diving so soon. Her cheeks had been flushed and her breathing a little erratic when he'd helped her into the truck. Still, she was a trooper, hanging in there for her friend.

She wouldn't stop until they found her friend. She reminded him of a bulldog—a pretty, petite Hawaiian bulldog with skin the color of mocha and eyes as dark as midnight. She'd taken time to tame her long black hair into a thick braid that hung halfway down her back, making her appear even younger and more vulnerable than the wild-eyed, crazy-haired female that had launched herself out of the back of an ambulance a few hours ago.

She sat in the seat beside him, her back straight, her eyes on the road ahead as they crossed to the opposite side of the island from the hospital and her home.

He didn't know much about her, other than she was an underwater photographer and she lived alone, based on what he'd observed in her house. There had been no signs of anyone but her living there. As pretty as she was, she had to have a boyfriend. Her ring finger was bare. Rex assumed that meant she was single. Yeah, he didn't know much about her.

"Is there anyone you need to call? Your folks, a boyfriend, fiancé, friends who might be worried about you?" He nodded toward his cell phone, where it lay in the cupholder. "You can use my phone."

Her brow furrowed. "My folks are dead. I already called Kalea after I called 911; she'll notify our friends. I don't have a boyfriend or fiancé."

"No?" He shot a glance her way.

"I know, right?" Her lips twisted into a wry grin. "What guy would pass up the opportunity to go out with a woman who'd rather be diving than drinking beer and watching football?"

"Not all men want a woman who drinks beer and watches football with them."

She shrugged. "I know. But I've been focused on building my business into something more than a hobby. I haven't met many guys willing to take the second stage to my work."

"And they shouldn't begrudge you that passion," Rex agreed.

"Through my work, I've established connections with local authorities and earned the permits needed to photograph in underwater nature preserves. It allows me to provide images to corporations keen to market the wonders of Hawaii. They don't hand out permits to just any photographer who wants to sell photographs commercially. I'm good at what I do. I wouldn't have been able to buy the equipment I use or qualify for a mortgage on my house if I weren't."

Rex gave her a nod. "Impressive."

"What about you?" Kimo asked. "While you're protecting me, is someone at home waiting for you?"

"I'm not married, if that's what you mean," he said.

She cocked an eyebrow toward him and gave him what he'd give her with a saucy, "No?"

He grinned, liking her sass and humor. "What woman could resist a man who preferred life in the military and being shot at to sitting behind a desk, day in and day out?"

"But you're not in the military anymore."

"When I was on active duty, it was easy to put serious relationships on hold when there were wars to fight. When I wasn't deployed, I trained. I never seemed to have the time...or the desire to commit to anyone."

"And now?"

Rex shrugged. "I have more time."

"But not the desire?" she finished for him.

"I gave my life to the Army. I never planned to marry and put a woman through the hassle and heartbreak."

"Again, you're not in the military anymore," Kimo persisted.

"I guess I haven't shifted my way of thinking after all those years abstaining from wedded bliss." Since coming home to Hawaii, he'd watched his teammates find love and embrace it with their whole hearts. The women they'd found weren't weak or defenseless, either. They could stand on their own and give as good as they got. His buddies were happier than he'd ever known them.

However, since his friends had found their women, they had less time to spend with him.

He didn't begrudge them the time they spent with their lovers, but it did leave him on his own more, to the point he was tired of his own company.

"Do you ever get lonely?" Kimo asked.

Damned if she hadn't hit the nail on the head with that question. Before he could think too hard on an answer, he admitted, "Sometimes."

As quickly as he'd answered, he continued, "With

my job, I meet new people, and I've been thinking of taking up a hobby."

"Oh, yeah? What?"

He hadn't really been thinking of taking up a hobby, but admitting to being lonely made him sound like a pathetic loser. "I don't know. Maybe driftwood carving, surfing, pickleball... I haven't decided."

"Pickleball?" Her eyebrows rose.

He frowned. "They have tournaments, you know. I've heard they might make it an Olympic event."

Kimo grinned. "I can't picture you playing pickleball. Now, surfing?" She gave him a considering glance. "Maybe. Driftwood carving? Can you sit still that long?"

His lips quirked. "No."

"What about diving?" she asked. "Have you?"

He nodded. "As a Delta Force Operator, we trained in diving and used those skills on a number of missions."

"Interesting." She tapped a finger to her chin. "So, you can be my dive partner when we go after that camera."

He nodded. "*If* we determine it's the only way to help us find your friend."

"Good to know. Though I'm an expert diver, I don't dive alone."

"Smart," he said. "You never know when you'll get into trouble."

Her lips firmed. "Like having someone purposely run you over with a boat or use you as target practice?"

"Yes," he said. "Or if you're attacked by a shark or get the bends."

"Turn left at the next road," Kimo said.

Rex made the turn.

While they'd been talking, they'd arrived at the other side of the island and were now driving along the road that led to the marina.

Kimo pointed at a shop across the street from the boat slips. A sign hung over the door proclaiming the store as Jako's Diving Adventures.

Rex parked in front of the shop and got out. He rounded the truck to help Kimo down, his hands resting around her waist a little longer than they probably should have. He blamed it on concern for her wounded leg.

"Steady?" he asked to cover for his lingering hold on her.

She looked up at him with those darker than dark eyes and nodded. "Steady as I can be. I have to break it to Jako that I lost his boat. He's not going to be happy."

"You didn't lose his boat. It was stolen," Rex reminded him. "Along with your friend."

"Yeah," she glanced toward the shop, her face grim. "But his boats are his livelihood."

Reluctantly, Rex released his hold on her waist and gripped one elbow. Just in case.

Kimo was completely capable of walking on her own, but she didn't shake loose of his grip until they entered the dive shop.

A young man with shoulder-length hair, wearing a Surf Hawaii T-shirt, stood in front of a row of scuba tanks, filling them one by one. When he spotted them, he straightened and brushed his hands across his swim trunks. "Hey, Kimo. What can I do to help you?"

"Hi, Sammie. I need to speak with Jako. Is he around?"

Sammie tipped his head toward the door they'd just come through. "He's across at the marina, servicing one of the dive boats."

"Thanks," Kimo said. "How's your mother getting around since her surgery?"

He grinned. "Better than she expected. She wishes she'd gotten her new hip sooner."

"Glad to hear that. She was in a lot of pain. Tell her I said hello and that I still want her recipe for jerk chicken."

"I will. Good to see you." Sammie went back to work, filling the tanks.

Kimo led the way through the door and across the street to the marina.

Rex followed, watching for any sign of trouble.

She stepped out on the dock, turned left and

walked past several boats where deckhands were cleaning after morning cruises, preparing for their next passengers to arrive.

Kimo stopped in front of a boat with a similar sign to the one over the dive shop: Jako's Diving Adventures. A man worked inside, positioning scuba tanks, BCDs, regulators, masks, snorkels and fins.

"Captain, permission to come aboard," Kimo called out.

The man set down the tank he held a little harder than was necessary. The shadow inside made his face impossible to read. "That you, Kimo?" he asked.

"It is," she responded, shading her eyes to peer into the darker interior of the dive boat.

Jako stiffened. "Get in here," he commanded in a rough tone.

Rex bristled and whispered to Kimo. "Maybe he should come out here."

"It's okay," she assured him and started toward the gangway.

Rex got there first and crossed onto the boat. He turned and held out a hand to Kimo.

She laid her hand in his palm and let him steady her as she crossed the same gangway.

Sure, she could do it on her own, but Rex wasn't taking any chances.

Once she was on the deck, he moved with her into the covered area.

"Jako, this is Rex Johnson, my...friend. He's been a big help to me after what happened last night."

"Jesus, Kimo, you're the last person I expected to see here." Jako took a step toward her.

Rex moved, positioning his own body between Jako and Kimo.

Jako glared at Rex and then turned his glare on Kimo and lowered his voice. "What the hell happened out there? I've heard everything from you and Alana crashing the boat into a reef, to you smuggling drugs using my boat. The Coast Guard showed up as I was opening, informing me that my boat had been reported missing. They asked if it had shown up here at the marina. Then, some detective with the Maui PD interrogated me like I'd murdered someone. Is it true that Alana is missing?"

"Oh, Jako." Kimo's eyes filled with tears. "Alana is missing. So, is your boat." She sat on a bench, tears streaming down her cheeks.

Jako sank onto the bench beside her as she told him what had happened.

"Why didn't you call me? I had to hear it all from the authorities. I was completely blindsided this morning."

"I'm sorry," Kimo said. "I should've called sooner. I'm really sorry about your boat. I hope they find it soon and that it's undamaged."

Jako shook his head. "Damn the boat. What are

they doing about Alana? And why couldn't they find that container when you gave them the coordinates?"

"The detective said they're looking into her disappearance." Kimo touched the man's arm. "I don't think they're moving fast enough. Worse, the Coast Guard reported that the container wasn't at those coordinates."

"You still using that dive watch I sold you?" Jako asked.

Kimo nodded. "I've never had a problem with it."

"It has the best ratings for its GPS capabilities." Jako shook his head. "Come to think of it, the Coastie and the detective didn't mention the container. They were all about the missing boat and then Alana."

"They probably think I was making it up, especially since they didn't find the container. I need to get out there and look for myself," Kimo said. "And I need to find the camera I was using. I took pictures of the container and what was inside." She shivered. "Jako, I need a favor."

Jako started shaking his head even before Kimo said, "I need a boat and dive gear."

Jako frowned. "Kimo, you know I'd do almost anything for you. We've been friends for a long time, but I can't give you a boat or gear."

Kimo's eyes widened. "What do you mean? I'll pay you for it—and I'll pay for your missing boat. I'll have to take out a loan, but I'll make it right."

He shook his head. "I can't rent you a boat. Before

I had a chance to call the insurance company to file a claim, they called me. They threatened to drop my coverage."

"I don't understand," Kimo said. "You pay for insurance to cover the loss of your boats. Why would they drop your coverage?"

"They threatened to drop my coverage if I rented so much as a snorkel to you."

"What?" Kimo jerked back as if Jako had slapped her. "Why?"

"They think you're responsible for Alana's disappearance and possible death. I told them they were crazy. Alana is your best friend. You two are inseparable."

"She is," Kimo whispered, her face pale, her eyes swimming. "We are. But they took her, and I have no idea where to look for her or who would do this." She gripped Jako's hands. "We have to find her before it's too late."

"I care about Alana as much as you do, but I've got employees who depend on my business to feed their families." He drew in a deep breath and let it out. "And there's more."

Rex wasn't sure how much more Alana could handle at this rate. He sat at her other side and laid a hand against her back. At that moment, he wished he could take away the pain, find her friend and fix everything wrong in her life.

Jako continued. "The bank that holds the mortgage on my business called after the insurance company and pretty much said the same. I'm not supposed to have anything to do with you until they figure out what really happened. That's why I was surprised to see you here. I thought they had already booked you and marched you off to jail."

Kimo shook her head. "They haven't yet, though the detective sure sounded like he believed I was guilty. I need a boat and gear. I have to get back out there and find the evidence I need to locate Alana and the people responsible."

Jako shook his head. "I can't give you the boat."

Kimo nodded. "I understand. You have to protect your business and the families who depend on it. I'll find another boat."

"Kimo, this is a small island. Word spreads fast. You might run into the same problem with the other dive companies."

Kimo's chin lifted. "I have to find Alana."

Rex leaned forward to meet Jako's gaze. "Do you have trackers on the boats you rent out to customers?"

Jako nodded. "I drop one into each boat when I rent it out to someone who isn't taking a member of my crew. I only check the location when the boat is late coming in. That way, if they've had engine trouble, I know where to find them." Jako stood and pulled his cell phone out of his pocket. "I have an app on my phone that I use to track them. I didn't think about it until just now."

Rex straightened and moved close enough to see the screen on the cell phone.

Kimo rubbed the tears from her cheeks. Rex curved a hand around her elbow and helped her rise. She stood beside Jako, tense, hopeful. "Can you get into the app? Maybe it'll give the boat's location."

She didn't say it, but Rex could almost hear her thinking that maybe the boat's location would lead them to Alana.

Jako clicked on an icon and waited. A login screen popped up. He scratched his head. "Now, which password did I use for this app?"

"Try something," Kimo urged.

"Give me a minute." He scratched his head again and then, using his thumbs, keyed something into the username and password fields and hit enter.

An error message appeared.

"Not that one. Let me try..." He keyed another username and password and hit enter. A churning circle appeared. Several seconds passed, and it was still churning.

"It would've displayed an error if it was the wrong password," Jako said. The screen chose that moment to present a map of Maui and a green dot.

Kimo leaned closer. "Where is it?"

Jako zoomed in on the dot and sighed. "It's right

here. It's the tracker for this boat. I just dropped the tracker on it this morning."

"Zoom out," Kimo said. "Maybe they left Maui for another island."

Jako zoomed out. "The trouble with the trackers is that they run out of battery." He shook his head. "It's not showing but let me look at its history. That's how I found one of my boats when the engine quit working." He fiddled with the app's options and brought up another screen with a green dotted line. "It displays the path the tracking device took." He pointed at the screen. "It started at the marina and went out into the Maalaea Bay."

"That was Alana and me. I bet if we compared the coordinates of the stop to my dive watch, they'd be really close." She held up her dive watch.

Jako zoomed in on the stop Alana and Kimo had made for their dive.

The coordinates were very close, but not the same. "Which makes sense. The coordinates I saved were for the shipping container. It wasn't in the same location as the boat, but it was close."

"The dotted line leads out of the bay, into the open ocean." Jako zoomed out to follow the line. "Then it disappears. The battery could have died."

"Or they could have scuttled the boat," Kimo said, her shoulders sagging.

"Looks like it could've been heading for either

Lanai or Molokai. We lost it as it was passing Kaho'olawe."

"We need to have someone check those islands to see if it ended up at one of them," Kimo said. "I still want to go back to the coordinates I saved for the container. Maybe there's something they missed when they extracted it. Then we can go from there to look for my camera."

"I'm sorry I can't help you," Jako said. "I've already lost one boat and a friend."

"I'll stay away until we find the proof we need that Alana was abducted and there was a container of dead people in Maalaea Bay."

"If you plan on going out anytime soon, be aware of that storm brewing in the Pacific. It's headed straight for the islands. It's supposed to be violent."

"I thought it was going to miss us," Kimo said.

Jako's lips pressed into a tight line. "It changed directions and is heading our way. I'm closing the shop the day after tomorrow. No boats will go out that day, even though it's not supposed to reach us until late that evening."

"We'll just have to find Alana before it hits." Kimo hugged Jako. "Again, I'm sorry."

He hugged her back. "Don't be. None of this is your fault. I'll let you know if I hear anything or if the boat turns up."

"Thank you, Jako."

"I hope you find Alana," he said.

"Me, too." Kimo turned away and walked across the deck.

Rex followed. When he came alongside her, he took her hand in his and helped her across the gangway onto the dock. Once there, he didn't let go. He gave her hand a gentle squeeze and said, "We'll find her." He didn't know how or when, but he'd do everything in his power to help her find her friend and justice for the people who'd died in the shipping container.

She looked up at him, her soulful dark eyes piercing his heart like nothing he'd ever felt before. Then her jaw hardened, and her fingers curled around his. "Yes. We will."

CHAPTER 7

KIMO LEFT JAKO, heartsick that one friend was still missing and another was being threatened. She went from one dive shop to the next, looking for anyone who would rent her the boat and gear she needed to conduct her own search for the container and her camera.

People she'd known for years told her the same story. Some appeared afraid of her, as if she'd already been tried and convicted of killing Alana.

She was leaving the last shop on the road in front of the marina when she practically ran into Dillon Bragg.

The man reached out and gripped Kimo's arms.

"Kimo," he said. "Babe. Long time no see."

Rex grabbed Dillon's shoulder, yanked him away from Kimo and then stood between them, snarling. "Back off."

Dillon backed a step and held up his hands. "Relax, man. I'm just greeting a friend." He glanced past Rex. Isn't that right, Kimo? Old friends. That's what we are."

Kimo shook her head. "It's okay, Rex. Dillon's not a threat." He was annoying as hell and had tried to get her to go out with him on multiple occasions. He couldn't understand that she had no desire to date the man or spend more than a few seconds at a time in his presence.

Rex remained positioned between Kimo and Dillon for a moment longer, his eyes narrowed.

Finally, he stepped back and crossed his arms over his chest in an intimidating stance.

"If you'll excuse us," Kimo said. "I'm kind of in a hurry."

"You know, no one's going to rent you a boat."

Kimo snorted. "I've figured that out."

"Maybe I could help," Dillon said. "I got a boat. I have no problem shuttling you around looking for mysterious containers."

Kimo wouldn't go out on any boat with Dillon. He was pushy, rude and sleazy around women in a way that made Kimo's skin crawl. She didn't trust the man. "Thanks, but I'll figure out something." She hooked her hand around Rex's arm and stepped past Dillon.

"The offer's open. I can get you out in a boat

sooner. Don't wait too long," Dillon called out behind them. "There's a storm headed our way."

Rex covered her hand with his and hurried her away. "Who was that man?"

"Dillon Bragg," Kimo murmured. "He thinks he's God's gift to women. Trust me, he's not. He's too handsy. Gives me the creeps. Thanks for not telling him I'm your client. He would take that as an invitation to continue bothering me."

Rex nodded. "After the trouble I had at the hospital, I thought it might be easier to keep the bodyguard/client thing on the downlow for the duration of our time together."

Kimo silently wondered how long their time together would be. She'd come to accept...no... *appreciate* having Rex at her side. After the attack and finding her home wrecked, Kimo didn't feel safe anywhere.

She had to remind herself that the man was her bodyguard. He'd leave when this whatever it was ended. She couldn't get too used to having him around. On that thought, she started to pull her hand out of the crook of her arm.

His fingers closed around hers, holding her hand in place. "Leave it there," he said softly.

"Why?" she asked, glad to hold onto him a little longer. "Do you think it makes people think we're together?"

"That, and I like it." He glanced down at her and winked.

Warmth spread through Kimo. For the first time in twenty-four hours, she smiled. "I like it, too."

With no other boat rental places in the marina area that would rent her the boat and gear she needed, they walked back down the length of the marina road.

"I feel naked," Kimo said as they neared the parking lot.

Rex's brow twisted. He shot a glance her way. "How so?"

"Well, maybe not naked, but missing things I'm used to having on me. I don't have my purse, my driver's license or my cell phone. Not to mention my keys were in my purse." She slowed as they approached her car, where she'd parked it the evening before in a parking area not far from Jako's Dive Adventures.

She reached out a hand to touch the Toyota Rav4.

"This yours?" Rex asked.

She nodded. "I bought it two years ago after I received a significant paycheck from a corporation that hired me to provide all their photographs for their resort marketing campaign. Alana and I have been all over the island in this car."

Her chest ached at the memory of her and Alana working the night before to unload her camera equipment from the rear of the SUV. They'd laughed again over a joke Leilani had told them at their last girls' night out with her and Kiana.

"Last night was supposed to be like any other night dive Alana had gone on with me. Only we were even more excited because the bioluminescence was supposed to be spectacularly evident. More brilliant. The conditions were perfect." She looked up into Rex's eyes. "And it was. The water was a magical blue. The sea life was active. We got some amazing pictures of turtles and an octopus Alana found on the reef."

Rex reached for her hand and held it in his. "We'll find her."

She gave him a smile she suspected was more of a grimace. "I hope we do before..."

He gave her fingers a gentle squeeze. "No negative thinking. Come on. There's got to be another boat rental place we can try."

He led her to the place they'd parked his truck in front of Jako's.

As he helped her up into the truck, his cell phone buzzed.

He didn't recognize the number but answered while standing in the doorway next to Kimo. "Rex here."

Kimo strained to hear the voice on Rex's cell phone. From what she could tell, it was female. A surprising stab hit square in her gut.

Though Rex had told her he wasn't married, he could be dating, which was absolutely his business.

Then why the knot in her gut? It wasn't like he belonged to her. Kimo had no hold on the man. He'd been hired to protect her. Nothing else.

Still, thinking of him with another woman felt...

He held out the cell phone. "It's for you. It's Leilani."

The knot in Kimo's gut loosened, and relief flooded her as she snatched his cell phone from his hand.

He left her with the cell phone and rounded the back of his truck to slide into the driver's seat.

Kimo swallowed hard and managed to eke out, "Leilani?"

"Girl! Why am I hearing second hand that you're in trouble and that our sweet Alana is missing? What the hell?" Leilani practically yelled.

"Oh, Leilani." Kimo's eyes filled, blurring her vision. "They took Alana." Tears slipped down her cheeks.

Leilani's voice softened. "Kalea told me. What can I do to help?"

Kimo scrubbed the tears from her cheeks and forced herself to think. "I need to go back to where we were diving."

"You can't do that. What if those men return?"

"I have to. I dropped my camera out there. It might have the clue I need to locate Alana."

"What clue?" Leilani asked.

"Did Kalea tell you about the shipping container?"

"She did," Leilani said. "Man, I can't imagine finding something that horrific. Those poor people."

"Did she tell you the Coast Guard didn't find the container?"

"Could they have been looking in the wrong place?"

Kimo shook her head. "I gave them the coordinates. I used those same coordinates to relocate it after surfacing for more air. It was there. I won't believe the Coast Guard can't locate a specific set of coordinates. They're trained to find people at specific locations. They didn't find it because it wasn't there. The container is gone."

"How will finding your camera help?"

"We took pictures of the container before and after we surfaced for fresh tanks. I hope there are some identification numbers on the container captured in the photographs. If there are, we might be able to trace the container to its owner. Maybe they'll lead us to who was out there in the same area —the people who attacked us and took Alana."

"What if it was stolen?" Leilani suggested.

"We'll have to figure it out from there. Photos of the container will prove it exists and that there were human bodies inside. I can't let their deaths go unnoticed. Someone chained them inside and dropped them in the ocean. Those people need to pay for doing that."

"You're right," Leilani agreed. "What are the police doing about it?"

"Nothing that I can tell. The detective on the case questioned me like I was the one who made Alana disappear."

"What the hell?" Leilani exclaimed. "You and Alana are as tight as sisters."

Kimo nodded. "We might as well be sisters. We've known each other and have been friends all our lives."

"If the police aren't taking your story seriously and the Coast Guard can't find the container, what can we do?"

Kimo's tears had dried, and her resolve stiffened. "I need to find my camera."

"You think you can?"

"I don't have a choice. I have to find it. I just know that the shipping container is connected to the people who took Alana. I think the same group is also the one that trashed my house. They're afraid someone will take me seriously and look for that container."

"They should take you seriously."

"Problem is, I can't get out there and dive without a boat and dive gear. Rumor has gotten out that I either abducted Alana or killed her and that I scuttled the boat to hide the evidence. No one will rent me a boat."

Leilani let out a long, low whistle. "No kidding?"

"No kidding. Jako's insurance company and bank got wind and threatened to cut him off if he did any business with me."

"That sounds like more than a rumor to me," Leilani said.

Kimo sighed. "Whatever it is, it's keeping me from getting back in the bay to look for my camera."

"You need a boat and diving gear?" Leilani asked.

"I do. My BCD and regulator are somewhere in Maalaea bay, as well as my camera."

"Kimo," Leilani said, dragging her name out, "what do I do for a living?"

"Take tourists on tours around the island," Kimo said.

"On land and in what?"

Kimo frowned. "A boat." She shook her head. "But you're not set up for diving. You don't rent all the equipment. You only take folks out to snorkel."

"I don't rent dive equipment, but I own some. And my boat will work as well as any Jako has for diving."

"Aren't you afraid your bank or insurance company will threaten to drop you if you help me?"

"Screw them," Leilani said. "You know me. I've been through the fires of hell and lived to tell about it. I'm not afraid of some silly bank executive or insurance salesman."

Hope swelled in Kimo's chest. "Can you loan me your boat?" She cast a glance toward Rex.

His eyebrows rose on his forehead.

"Not only can I loan you a boat, but I can also drive it and dive with you."

A frown pulled at Kimo's brow. "I can't ask you to go along. Those same people who attacked us the first time might come after me again."

"Then I'll bring my own personal bodyguard, Angel. I hear Rex was assigned to you. According to my guy, you'll like him. He's the strong, serious type. But I get the feeling he's got a heart of gold beneath his stoic exterior."

Kimo's cheeks heated as she glanced toward Rex, hoping he couldn't hear Leilani's description of him. She'd nailed it. Rex was the strong, serious type. And he had given her a glimpse of the heart inside when he'd come to her defense while the detective had been ass and when Dillon had gotten in her space. But it was when he'd held her hand after that last encounter that she'd seen his softer side.

Her fingers were still warm from contact with his.

Kimo forced herself to focus on her mission, not the man sitting patiently in the driver's seat. "Still, I'm worried about how dangerous it will be. One of my friends is missing. I'd hate to lose another."

"I insist," Leilani said. "And having two Brotherhood Protectors will add to the safety of your effort. We might even ask Hawk to send a couple more.

We'll each need a dive buddy and a couple of armed men on the boat to protect the area around the boat."

Kimo really didn't want another friend to potentially risk her life. "I don't have many options with word spreading that I lost a dive buddy and a boat."

Rex leaned over the console and pointed at the cell phone. "Put her on speaker."

"Hold on." Kimo stared into Rex's eyes. "Rex wants in on the conversation."

"Good," Leilani said. "He needs to be."

Kimo handed the cell phone over to Rex.

He put the call on speaker. "Leilani, I gather you're proposing taking one of your tour boats?"

"That's right. One of my boats and me," she answered. "But considering what happened to Kimo and Alana, I'll bet money Angel won't let me go without him, nor would I want to. I think we'll need more than just me and Kimo to make this happen."

"I agree," Rex said. "I'll contact Hawk and see if any other members of our team are available to accompany us. What timeframe are we aiming for?"

Kimo held Rex's gaze across the cell phone. "As soon as possible."

"Two of our boats are out on tour as we speak and won't be back until this afternoon. The third one is in the shop for maintenance. I can have a boat ready by five this afternoon. If you find one to rent sooner, you won't hurt my feelings. But I'm going with you either way, as will Angel and Rex."

Kimo wanted to get out there sooner rather than later that afternoon. "Okay. I'll let you know if I find another boat. Thanks, Leilani, for being my friend and being you."

"I love you, Kimo. Let's find Alana and bring her home. Now, I'd better get to work. I'll have to service the dive gear and stage it for our dive. One other thing, since you're poison to all the boat rentals and dive shops, you might want to come in disguise."

"Good idea," Kimo said. "That'll help keep your reputation out of hot water."

"And maybe distract whoever is out to trash you and your reputation," Leilani said. "Keep me in the loop." She ended the call.

"Sounds like we have a boat," Rex said.

Kimo nodded. "I want to look a little more for a rental. I don't like waiting that long to do something about finding Alana."

"We can do that," he said.

"First, I'd like to get a replacement phone with my own number. I can't keep relying on yours."

"I don't mind loaning you mine."

"People who don't know I'm with you won't be able to get a hold of me. Like Leilani. If she hadn't gotten a call from Kalea, she wouldn't have known how to get in touch with me." Kimo waved a hand. "I run a business with customers expecting me to answer my phone. Some of the data I lost was supposed to go to those customers in the next few days. Not that I give a damn about those orders when Alana is who knows where."

Rex reached out and took her hand. "Okay. Let's go get you a phone."

Rex drove back across the island to the store where Kimo had purchased her old cell phone.

After almost an hour, Kimo walked out of the store with a shiny new cell phone Rex had loaned her money to buy. Though she hated being beholden to the man, at least she was back online, able to connect with friends and clients. Once in Rex's truck, she checked her text messages and found several from her corporate customers.

As Kimo read the first one, her heart sank to her knees. "The rumors have spread all the way to Oahu."

"What do you mean?" Rex asked.

"My representative from the resort that contracted me to provide photos for their new marketing campaign texted me." She shook her head. "He says that based on information he received today about what happened last night and suspicion pointing to me as responsible for Alana's disappearance, he regrets to inform me that he's cancelling the contract." She looked up, meeting Rex's gaze, the hand holding her new phone trembling. "I was going to send them the files tomorrow. It was done. I only held onto it for maybe one more photo including the bioluminescence."

"You're being tried and found guilty by whoever

is spreading the rumors. News reporters haven't beaten down your door for the story. You'd think they would be the ones broadcasting that kind of news. I'll have Swede look into the source."

Kimo glanced back at her cell phone and gasped at the next text. "And here's another cancellation. The client stated pretty much the same thing." She scrolled through two more texts, her stomach roiling. She switched to voicemail and found another customer who'd left her a message to cancel a photo-shoot she'd scheduled for her business. These were the kinds of accounts that kept her in business. Without them, she'd lose everything. "My customers are bailing on me."

"All the more reason to find someone to rent you a boat and get back out in the bay to find that camera," Rex said. "Who else can you call for a boat rental?"

Kimo spent the next hour calling every boat-rental place she could find.

Rex texted Swede and then drove to the gas station to fill his tank.

No one would rent her a boat. When she'd exhausted all possibilities, she laid her phone in her lap. "As soon as I say my name, they say no. I don't even get to ask them if they have a boat to rent."

Rex had just pulled into a drive-thru of a fast-food restaurant and ordered two burgers fully loaded with fries and sodas.

"Let me try." Rex picked up his cell phone. Before he could place a call, Kimo laid a hand on his arm.

"Don't bother," she said. "We have a boat at five. That's only an hour away."

"Okay, then. Now that that's settled..." He pulled forward, paid for their meal, handed her the bag, stuck the drinks in the truck's cupholders and drove the truck into an empty parking lot. "Let's eat."

He handed her a burger and an order of fries. "Sorry. I didn't ask if you wanted a burger or something else."

She took the hamburger with a grateful smile. "It's not the time to worry about eating healthy. Besides, they make the best burgers in town." She peeled back the wrapper. "As long as it has pickles, I'm in."

"It's fully loaded, including the pickles," he said.

"Perfect." Though her stomach was still knotted with concern for her friend, she bit into the burger anyway. It was so good she ate half of it before she gave up and picked at the fries. "Thanks," she said.

Rex swallowed the last bite of his burger. "For what?"

"Taking care of me. I hadn't even thought about eating since Alana disappeared."

"I call it self-preservation." He lifted his soda. "We have to keep up our strength, especially if we're diving this evening." He held his cup up. "To finding the camera."

She tapped her cup to his. "To finding Alana."

He nodded. "To Alana." He took a sip from his straw. "Do you think your customers will come back when they learn you weren't responsible for Alana's disappearance?"

"I don't know." She'd been sick after getting all the calls and texts from her clients cancelling orders. "After the shock, I'm angrier than anything else. None of that matters if Alana doesn't come home. Screw those customers."

At that moment, Rex's cell phone chirped. He glanced at the screen. "It's Swede. Let's hope he's found something we can use."

Kimo crossed her fingers in her lap. It was a silly gesture and probably wouldn't affect the outcome of Swede's search at all, but she was running out of ideas.

Rex answered the call and put the cell phone on speaker. "You're on speaker with Kimo and me. What have you got?"

"Good," Swede said. "I have Hawk on the call as well. I thought he'd like to hear what I've found."

"Hey, Rex. Kimo," Hawk said. "Go ahead, Swede."

"First, there was one short news announcement about a woman who went missing during a night dive on Maui," Swede said. "No mention of her name or of Kimo."

Kimo frowned. "If it wasn't in the news, how did my customers link my name to Alana's disappearance? I can't believe the gossips would bother to call the companies I've been working with to point their fingers at me. It doesn't make sense."

"And how did every boat rental company on Maui suddenly learn of the incident and block Kimo from renting?" Rex added.

"Unless they have one hell of a grapevine on Maui, you're right," Hawk said. "It doesn't make a whole lot of sense."

"Maui is a small island. Most of the locals know each other, but it's still a stretch to get to every boat rental company," Kimo murmured. "Thankfully, I have a friend who's coming through for us."

"That's right," Rex said. "We're heading out at five with Leilani and Angelo Cortez."

"I was able to get Devlin Mulhaney and Teller Osgood on standby, waiting for instructions on where to meet," Hawk said.

Rex frowned. "I thought Teller was on the Big Island."

"He was," Hawk said. "I sent him to Maui on a flight on the off chance you might need him."

"We'll need him," Rex confirmed. "Dev and Teller can cover us from the boat while Kimo, Angel, Leilani and I search for the camera." He turned to Kimo. "If that's all right with you."

She nodded. "It is, as long as everyone understands the danger that could be involved. Especially if those men show up again."

Rex gave Kimo a brief nod. "Speaking for my team, we do."

"It's what we do," Hawk reinforced.

Feeling a little better with food in her stomach and backup for the dive, Kimo nodded. "Then we meet at Leilani's slip at Lahaina Harbor at five."

"Now that you have that settled," Swede said, "I have another piece of information for you."

Kimo held her breath, praying it was good news, not more of the bad stuff.

"Kimo, you'll be happy to know I was able to recover your files from your online storage site."

She let her breath out in a woosh. "Really?"

"Really," he said. "Not only that, but I also found the photo of the container that you uploaded and was able to locate an identification number."

"Were you able to trace it to the company that owned it?" Rex asked.

"I was," Swede said. "It's owned by Holte Maritime Group, a shipping corporation operating out of the west coast of the US with a corporate headquarters on Oahu."

Rex frowned. "Marcus Holte is the owner."

Kimo glanced across at him. "You know him?"

"I know of him. He and my father were business associates. At least, they were when I was younger. They attended some of the same events. Galas, charity auctions, state functions."

"I looked him up," Swede said. "He's highly

regarded in the industry and seems to run a clean operation, following all the maritime laws and has a pretty healthy philanthropic reputation."

"Were you able to tap into their cargo manifests to locate that particular shipping container?" Hawk asked.

"I was," Swede said. "It's supposed to be on a ship enroute to Hong Kong. I tracked the ship it was supposed to be on. The route originated from the Port of San Francisco, with a stop in Kaumalapau on Lanai three days ago, then on to Hong Kong, which it should reach in fifteen or twenty days. The ship would have offloaded or taken on more cargo on the west side of Lanai and wouldn't have passed between Lanai and Maui or anywhere close to Maalaea Bay."

"Which means that container was offloaded at the port in Lanai," Rex said. "But by whom and onto what?"

"The cargo manifest didn't show the container as having been offloaded. It's supposed to be on that ship to Hong Kong."

"Heading toward the storm that's supposed to hit Hawaii two days from now," Hawk said, "where they could legitimately say the container was lost at sea."

"Did you find out who managed the offloading of the containers on Lanai?" Hawk asked.

"Yes," Swede said. "Again, Holte Maritime Group."

"We need to talk to Marcus Holte," Hawk said.

"I tried to set up a meeting with Mr. Holte,"

Swede said, "but he didn't have anything available until next week."

"That's too late," Kimo said. "Alana might not have that kind of time left."

"Swede, see what you can find about Holte's whereabouts. Maybe we can crash one of his meetings," Hawk said. "I'll send someone to Lanai to poke around the harbor and ask questions of the stevedores who unload the ships."

Kimo's head spun with what they'd just learned. Only one thing was clear. "Knowing who owns the container isn't necessarily leading us to Alana."

"Not yet," Swede said. "We have to find the people responsible for offloading that container. If it's not Holte's operation, who stepped in to reroute it? Whoever that is will be in charge of the thugs who came after you and Alana."

"Like I said," Hawk continued, "I'll send someone to the harbor on Lanai to ask around."

"Is it possible to track the smaller vessels that might've shown up in the harbor at the same time as the ship carrying Holte's container?" Rex asked.

"I'm working on that," Swede said. "Based on the Harbor Master's records, there were a number of smaller vessels owned by various individuals and corporations. I'll be sorting through them to look for any connections between them and the Holte Maritime Group."

"In the meantime, Kimo, we still need your

camera," Hawk said. "It's the only proof that people were inside that container."

Rex met Kimo's gaze and responded for them with, "We'll be out there this evening."

"I hope you find your camera," Swede said. "It might be the only way to help those people find justice."

"Right back atcha," Kimo said. "We need the connection between the Holte's container ship and whoever received it. Those people have to be the ones who have Alana."

"I'm working on it and hope to have it soon," Swede assured them. "For now, out here." Swede left the call.

"Rooster and Reid are flying over from Oahu to Lanai to talk with the stevedores who work the cargo operations at the harbor there," Hawk said. "I'll let you know what they find as soon as I hear anything. If that's all for now, I'm out here."

Hawk ended the call.

Kimo's cell phone buzzed with an incoming text.

She glanced down at the message, expecting it to be from Leilani or Hawk with further instructions. The call was from neither of those people. The caller ID was Unknown.

As she read the words, all the air left Kimo's lungs.

Unknown: Your camera for your friend.

CHAPTER 8

WHAT?" Rex leaned over the console to stare down at Kimo's cell phone screen.

"They want my camera," Kimo whispered, her face pale. "That means they know I have proof of what was inside that container." She glanced up at Rex. "The only way they could know that is if Alana told them."

"She's alive," Rex said. "They wouldn't use her as a bargaining chip if she wasn't."

Kimo's eyes swam with tears. "She's alive."

Rex wanted to pull her into his arms, but the console sat between them. As he thought about the message, his brow dipped. "That text probably came from a burner phone, given it's an unknown caller ID. Text them back and demand proof of life."

Kimo held her phone in front of her, her fingers poised over the screen. "What do I say?"

"Tell them to give you proof that Alana is alive."

Kimo's hand shook as she keyed the message. She had to back up several times to correct the spelling when she hit the wrong keys. When she'd entered Rex's exact words, she met his gaze.

After he gave her a brief nod, she sent the message. For a long moment, she stared at the screen, waiting for that proof.

As a minute passed, then another, her concentration never wavered.

When her cell phone chirped, she jerked and almost dropped the device.

"It's a video," she said and clicked on the image.

The feed blinked into view with a video of a blond-haired woman with brown eyes.

"It's Alana," Kimo said, her voice cracking.

"Kimo, whatever they want, don't do it," she said.

A hand lashed out, backhanding Alana across her face. Her head jerked back.

"Alana!" Kimo cried.

Alana sagged forward. The camera remained on the blonde as a disembodied voice said, "The camera for your friend. Or she ends up like the others."

Kimo keyed into the phone.

Kimo: If my friend dies, the camera and the images on it will go directly to the police

Unknown: If the images get out, your friend dies. No negotiation

"Can you play the video again in slow motion?" Rex asked.

"I can try." Kimo pressed the play arrow.

Rex focused on the background behind Kimo's friend.

"What are you looking for?" Kimo asked.

"Anything that could be a clue as to where they're keeping her."

Kimo leaned close, studying the video as well.

"Looks like they're keeping her in a small room with a low ceiling and dim lights," Rex said. "The wall appears clean and white, not made of drywall or tile."

"Looks like what they use on the insides of a boat cabin," Kimo said. "But I don't see anything else. No signs or letters on the walls to indicate a make or model of the craft. She could be on a number of different kinds of boats, including a catamaran or yacht."

Whoever had been manning the camera had zoomed in on Alana, making it hard to see much more of the room. Most of the view was filled with Alana's bruised and pale face. She appeared to be sitting in a chair, her hands secured behind her back.

Kimo winced as the hand lashed out, smacking Alana in the face.

"Pause," Rex said.

Kimo paused the video with the arm still extended.

Kimo pointed. "Is that a tattoo?"

Rex nodded.

Kimo zoomed in on the tattoo. "Looks like a stylized tribal mask." Her eyes widened. "I've seen something similar."

Rex nodded. "Members of my team ran into guys with those tattoos on Oahu. They belonged to a motorcycle gang that goes by the name of Order of the Demons."

"Holy shit," Kimo whispered. "They're known to be ruthless."

"Yeah." He leaned back. "I need to stop by my apartment to collect some of my dive equipment, and I'd like to make a call from there. We can share the video with my tech guru. He can run a check on it and see if he can come up with any more information Alana's location."

Kimo nodded. "You could drop me at my place. I need to clean up."

Rex shook his head. "Not a chance I'm dropping you anywhere. You're stuck with me for the duration of this situation. Besides, we don't have much time."

"I think you have it backward," Kimo said with a grimace. "*You're* stuck with *me*." She held up a hand. "I know, it's your job."

Rex nodded. He didn't want to admit it was quickly becoming more than just a job. The pretty Hawaiian was a strong, independent woman who'd survived a pretty traumatic event and didn't want to leave her friend behind. She was more than adamant about finding her, even if she had to do it all by herself. She reminded him of someone he'd loved.

He shifted into gear and pulled out of the parking lot. "You remind me of my mother."

Kimo laughed. "I consider myself fairly young still, and I haven't found my first gray hair." She shook her head with a twisted smile. "I don't know whether to be flattered or insulted."

Rex smiled. "Flattered. My mother put up with a lot being married to my father. She always supported his work and career without complaint, while he didn't really seem to see her. Her passion was helping others. She volunteered in women's shelters and visited children in the cancer treatment hospitals. She helped raise money for both organizations and would've given the shirt off her back to a stranger or a homeless person."

"From all you've said about her, she sounds pretty amazing," Kimo said.

Rex's heart pinched hard in his chest. "She was."

"How did she die?" Kimo asked. "If you don't mind my asking."

"One of the women she'd befriended at the women's shelter had retrained to become a nurse and was working shiftwork at one of the bigger hospitals on Oahu when she came down with a particularly bad case of the flu. She stayed home from work too long when she should've gone to the hospital." Rex shook his head. "When my mother heard she was sick, she went to the woman's apartment, took her soup, fed and cared for her until she realized she wasn't getting better. Finally, she called an ambulance. They took her to the hospital, got her on antibiotics and a ventilator. It was touch-and-go for a while, but she got better."

"And your mother?"

"She got the same flu but didn't tell anyone. Didn't go to the hospital. My father was away on a business trip. Our housekeeper was on vacation. By the time the housekeeper returned, my mother was already in organ failure."

Kimo's brow furrowed. "Did you get back to see her before...?"

Rex nodded. "Barely. I spent the last few hours with her. She could barely talk but seemed to want to get some things off her chest."

"Is that when she told you not to let anyone take your choices away?"

"Yes," Rex said. "She'd studied to be a social worker. When she married my father, she gave up her own career to support his. After I was old enough that I didn't need her at home, she threw herself into helping others. She didn't regret raising me, though I could be a challenge at times, especially when I butted heads with my father. I always thought it was because I was too much like him—hardheaded and always thinking I was right."

"I don't see that," Kimo said. "I think you're more

like your mother than you realize. You care about your team. You're working as hard as I am to find Alana, a woman you don't know. You're taking good care of me, another woman you don't know, and you care about the people who died in that shipping container."

He gave her a sideways glance. "You're too kind—like my mother. However, now that I've been away from my father for over a decade, I've realized I'm not like him. He's completely driven by the almighty dollar. His focus was never on his family but on how to grow his business and increase his profits each year. He didn't even get back from his business trip until the day after my mother passed."

Kimo reached over and touched Rex's arm. "That's sad."

Rex gave a bark of laughter that was anything but joyful. "Get this. My mother told me to tell my father that she forgave him for not making it back in time. That she would be all right."

"What did he say when you told him that?"

Rex snorted. "He said, '*Well, okay then. Have you had dinner?*'"

"Wow." Kimo blinked. "Was he not upset or anything?"

"I don't know." Rex drew in a deep breath and let it out. "I turned and walked away. He handed her funeral over to a service. I went back to our house, packed a few of my belongings, my passport and birth certificate and then marched down to the nearest recruiting station, which happened to be the Army's, and signed up. My father called to ask where I'd gone. I told him. He said that if I didn't go back to school and finish my degree, he'd disown me."

"That's harsh," Kimo said, "especially after losing your mother. So, he disowned you?"

"I don't know. Don't care." Rex stared at the road ahead. "I didn't want anything to do with him after that. Since he paid for the phone, I tossed it in the trash. I didn't need one in basic training anyway." After spilling his guts to a woman who was practically a stranger, Rex was stunned at how easy it was to talk with Kimo. He'd never told another soul about his family situation. He'd never gotten close enough to a female to want to.

Kimo sat back in her seat. "Wow. That makes my childhood sound like a picnic. My mother and father were always loving and happy to be with each other and me. They took me to all the island's cultural events to teach me about my Hawaiian heritage. We stuck together as a family when the fires drove us out of our home in Lahaina and worked to rebuild our lives in the aftermath."

"I heard about the fires. That had to be hard," he said.

She nodded. "The community came together to lift each other up. And we came through. Battered, but not beaten."

"That shows your resilience as a people."

"Some things you can come back from," she said softly.

"What happened with your folks?"

She stared out the side window. "They were flying to Kauai for their thirtieth wedding anniversary. I'd paid for them to stay in a swanky resort with one of the largest paychecks I'd earned for photographs and a video I'd produced for a major resort chain. They'd sprung for a charter flight with a friend who flew celebrities to the different islands." She paused, still looking out the side window.

Rex shot a glance toward her.

By the reflection in the window, it was clear she was fighting back tears.

A lump formed in Rex's throat. He felt her loss like an echo of the pain he'd felt when his mother had taken her last breath, and her hand had gone limp in his. He'd been alone, much like Kimo had been. No other family to console him. His father, a cold, heartless bastard, had done nothing to help him through or even share in the pain.

Rex reached for Kimo's hand and held it without pressing for more information.

Her fingers curled around his. After a moment, she brushed a tear from her cheek. "You'd think after a year and a half, I wouldn't still get choked up telling the story."

"I still get choked up. It's been thirteen years. I still cry on my mother's birthday," he said.

She looked up at him, her brow wrinkling. "I can't imagine you crying about anything."

His lips pressed together. "That would be my father."

"And you're not like him," she said with a nod.

"Not as much as I used to think." He continued to drive, holding her hand in his.

He liked how soft yet strong her fingers were. As an expert diver, she wasn't a sissy or weak in any way. She was smart, creative and cared deeply about others. She'd cried several times since he'd taken her on as a client, but it was because of the loss of loved ones. Though she'd cried, she hadn't stopped looking for a way to save her friend.

"The plane was a single-engine prop job. The FAA investigation reported that they'd likely had a bird strike the propeller. Another hit the windscreen. They were already coming down when it happened. The pilot probably couldn't see, and they were too low to recover or find a place to land. They crashed into the ocean. They died on impact."

Rex squeezed her hand gently without saying a word.

She stared at their joined hands for a long moment. "Thank you."

He looked her way. "For what?"

"For not saying *at least they died instantly.*" She gave

him a watery smile. "So many people said that to the point I wanted to scream that they shouldn't have died at all. If I hadn't paid for the vacation on Kauai, they would've stayed home and celebrated as usual at our favorite restaurant." She shook her head. "I was so proud of making enough money to treat them."

"You couldn't have known a bird would crash into the plane. It wasn't your fault," he said softly. "They could've been run over by a bus crossing the road to your favorite restaurant. It's probably even more likely for that to happen than for a plane to crash."

"I know, but it happened to my parents and the pilot. I still feel guilty. And I feel just as guilty and responsible for Alana's abduction."

"You didn't abduct her, Kimo," he said softly. "Those men who attacked you two did it."

She nodded. "I know. It doesn't change how I feel."

As they approached town, she pointed to a store in a strip mall. "There's a beachy souvenir shop. I need a disguise. I bet I can find one in there."

Rex pulled into the parking lot and shifted into park. When he went to open his door, she put a hand on his arm.

"You don't have to go in. I'm sure there aren't any bad guys in there. They wouldn't guess we'd stop here."

"True." He covered her hand with his briefly. "But I'm not letting you out of my sight for a minute.

You're the only one who might know where to look for that camera. That means you have a big target on your back to bury those images, and you. And if they get to you before you get to the camera..."

"They have no reason to keep Alana alive." She nodded. "Come on, BG, let's get in and out so we can move on to the next phase of this operation."

Rex grinned. "Look at you sounding all military."

Her lips twitched. "I couldn't help it. Seems like we're a stealth operation on the move." Her smile spread. "Into a souvenir shop. Go figure. I need you anyway. Since I don't have a purse, I can't pay for this disguise. Can you spot me for the amount? I can pay you back once I can get into my bank account."

"No problem." As he opened the door to the store, he asked, "BG? Is that for bodyguard?"

"No, silly. It stands for Big Guy." She ducked past him into the store, her smile still on her lips.

She was a beautiful woman, her Hawaiian heritage making her even more exotic and attractive. And when she smiled, the sun shone brighter.

Rex found his step lighter as he followed her through the store where she chose a beach cover-up, flip-flops, sunglasses and a floppy hat.

"This ought to do it. I'll look like any other customer on one of Leliani's snorkeling trips." She laid the items on the counter.

"What, no swimsuit?" Rex asked.

"I'm wearing one under my clothes," she pulled

the collar of her shirt to one side, displaying the strap of her bikini.

"You came prepared."

Her lips pressed together. "I'd hoped to be out on the water a lot sooner."

"We'll be out there soon," he assured her and paid for the items. He gathered the bag and took the receipt from the clerk.

Once outside the store, Kimo reached out a hand. "I'll take that receipt. I intend to repay you for lunch, my phone and my disguise."

He hesitated. "That's not necessary. It wasn't that much."

"I insist," she said. "I'm not a freeloader."

He shook his head. "Didn't say you were." Though he didn't like doing it, he handed her the receipt and held her door open.

As she climbed into his truck, she stared down at him, holding the door for her. "Since so many people have seen me with you, you might consider a disguise of your own."

"I have something I can use at my apartment. I won't take long." He closed the door and rounded to the driver's side.

Once he settled behind the wheel, he drove to his apartment and backed into a parking space. He'd watched in his rearview mirror and along the sides of the road for anyone who might be tailing them. So far, he hadn't spotted any suspicious activity. When he got out of the truck, he hurried around to the passenger side and helped Kimo down, using his body as a shield. He didn't think anyone had followed him, but if they knew he was with her, they could have someone staking out his apartment.

"We have just enough time to change and get over to the marina in Lahaina," Kimo said as she entered his apartment.

After he closed the door and twisted the lock,

Rex pointed to a door off the small living area. "You can have the front bathroom while I change in my room."

Kimo ducked in and closed the door behind her.

Rex stared at the door for a moment, amazed at the woman's resilience. She should be exhausted and ready to collapse. Instead, she was chomping at the bit to get out on the water, find her camera and save her friend.

Yes, she was like his mother in some ways. Kind, caring, strong.

Still, he didn't feel at all like Kimo's son. Quite the opposite, in fact. He found himself wanting to pull her into his arms, and not in a brotherly way.

Something about Kimo made his blood stir in a way no other woman ever had.

"I'll be ready in two minutes," Kimo called out through the bathroom door.

Aware he had more changing to do than she did, Rex hurried into his room, leaving the door slightly ajar. As he crossed to his dresser, he kicked off his shoes, shucked his jeans and pulled his shirt over his head.

He dug into the bottom drawer for the loud green and yellow swim trunks he'd bought to go with an equally obnoxious Hawaiian shirt.

Once he was suitably dressed, he dug in his dive bag, located his dive watch, snorkel and mask. He'd use the regulator and tanks Leilani was to provide, but he liked his watch. Angel had one like it, too. They'd be able to perform basic communications between them while underwater.

After checking the battery charge, he slipped the watch onto his wrist and emerged from the bedroom, carrying his snorkel and mask.

Kimo had pulled her hair up and tucked it beneath the floppy hat, hiding it completely. The beach cover-up hung open, revealing a bright red bikini that complemented her dark, Hawaiian skin tones. Yes, he'd seen her naked in the dark reflection on the hospital monitor, but seeing her gorgeous body peeking through the cover-up, her luscious breasts pushed up by the bikini top...

Rex's groin tightened. "Uh." He cleared his throat. "Great disguise."

As Kimo's gaze swept over him head to toe, Rex moved his mask to cover that part of him that was having a purely involuntary reaction to her.

Kimo's widened, and she blinked, grinning. "You

look like a pineapple plantation and a neon green paint factory exploded on you."

"Thanks," he grimaced. "I thought it looked touristy."

"It looks something," she said. "You bought that outfit?"

"In my defense, the guys pranked me."

Kimo walked around him, studying his choice of beachwear. "I gotta hear this."

"I was invited to a Christmas party at the Swaying Palms Resort, where Devlin's woman, Kiana, worked."

"Kiana's my friend. I was invited to that party, too, but couldn't make it at the last minute because I came down with the flu."

"You didn't miss anything. They'd told me it was mandatory to wear an ugly Hawaiian outfit as there would be a contest, the Hawaiian version of an Ugly Christmas Sweater contest. I showed up in this with matching neon green flipflops and neon green-rimmed sunglasses."

Her brow furrowed. "I thought the dress code for that event was business casual and cocktail attire."

His lips twisted. "It was."

Kimo laughed. "Now, I have to get copies of the pictures from Kiana. That's hilarious."

He grimaced. "Maybe to you and my supposed friends."

"What have you done to prank them back?" she asked as she headed for the door.

"Nothing, yet. Still working on it." He grabbed his keys, sunglasses and a neon green fisherman's hat from a hook on the wall. He plunked the hat on his head and opened the door. "Let me check the parking lot first."

She nodded, her floppy hat bobbing.

Rex stepped out in his outlandish getup, scanned the parking area and the bushes and trees surrounding it. Nothing moved in the shadows. No different cars had arrived in the lot since he'd parked. "All clear," he said and turned to take her hand. "But stay close to me."

Kimo frowned. "Do you think we're being stalked?"

"I'd rather act like we're being followed than be surprised," he said.

Kimo poked her head, floppy hat and all, out the door, looked right, then left and finally stepped out. She let him slip an arm around her and hustle her out to his truck, up and in. Once she was in her seat, she scrunched low until her head barely showed through the window.

Rex rounded to the driver's side and slipped in behind the wheel. He didn't say anything as he drove out of the parking lot and onto the road leading to the marina at Lahaina.

"Turn here," Kimo said. "We can zigzag through

the streets in case anyone is following us. Maybe even turn around and head back a couple of streets before we continue to Lahaina."

Rex's lips quirked. "I like the way you think."

"I have to admit," she said. "The fact that if something happens to us before we find the camera affects what happens to Alana scares me even more. I'm glad I have you to protect me—for Alana's sake."

"And yours," he added softly. Once on the highway, heading for Lahaina, Rex checked the rearview mirror.

Kimo turned in her seat as well. "I don't see anyone following us."

"Same." He hadn't had time to call his father while they'd been in his apartment. He wanted to ask if he knew anything about Marcus Holte. He pulled out his cell phone and dialed the one number he'd saved but hadn't used in thirteen years. He'd only saved it so that he'd know who it belonged to when, or if, it ever came across on his screen. That way, he could ignore the call and get on with his life as usual.

When his team had decided to come to Hawaii, he'd balked. He'd joined the Army to leave the islands and his father behind. Being back had been difficult at first. It took him a while to realize he didn't have to see the man or interact with him, especially since he was on Oahu and Rex was on Maui.

Sure, he might have assignments that would take him to Oahu. With a population of nearly one million people and many more tourists, the chances of running into the man were slim to none.

If not for Kimo and her friend Alana, Rex wouldn't bother to call his father. For them, he'd call. His father might know more about Holte Maritime Group, and in particular, Marcus Holte.

The phone rang three times before a gruff voice answered, "Who the hell's calling and who gave you this number?"

Rex drew in a deep breath and pushed the past behind him. He needed answers.

CHAPTER 9

Rex sat stiffly behind the wheel, negotiating the speed and turns with one hand while he held the cell phone in the other.

Kimo couldn't look away from him as he placed the phone call.

Who was he calling that made him so tense?

"James Johnson?" Rex asked, his voice tight. "It's Rex Johnson. Your son."

The air left Kimo's lungs. He was calling his father. The man he hadn't talked to since his mother's death.

She strained to hear the other end of the call as Rex pushed on.

"I don't want to bother you, but it's a matter of life and death." Rex paused to listen. "Yes. That's what I said. Life or death. I remember you knew Marcus

Holte of Holte Maritime Group, and I'm not talking about his life or death." He paused and listened.

Rex was calling his father about Holte. Kimo struggled even harder to listen to the other end of the conversation.

She couldn't make out more than a gruff tone barking across the line into Rex's ear.

Rex let the man talk for a few more seconds. Then he cut in with, "I need to know if he's on the up and up, or if he's into shady shipping practices."

The barking started all over again.

"No, it's not a matter of life and death for me." He listened, his lips pressed into a thin line. "Look, if you don't know anything about him, I'll let you get back to whatever you were doing." Rex started to lower his cell phone.

"James Rex Johnson, Jr.!" the voice on the line shouted. "Don't you hang up on me!"

He raised the phone to his ear. "I'm listening."

Rex's father stopped shouting, his voice now nothing but a murmur to Kimo.

She sat with her hands twisting the fabric of her cover-up, wishing Rex had put the call on speaker because she was dying to know what the other man was telling him.

"I got that from the internet. Clean record, philanthropist to his favorite charities. That's not what I'm looking for. Do you know if he's been involved in any illegal shipments or cargo?"

Kimo held her breath, wishing she could hear the other man's answer.

"That's all you've got? Untouchable?" Rex shook his head. "What exactly does that mean?"

What did that mean? Kimo frowned, her thoughts spinning. Who was untouchable? Holte or Rex's father? Untouchable by whom?

"I see," Rex said, his jaw so tight a muscle twitched in his cheek. "No, I won't be calling again soon. If you remember anything more substantial, you can text or call me. I need that information soon. Again, life or death."

Rex ended the call and threw his cell phone into the cupholder.

Kimo gave him a minute or two to calm down before she tentatively asked, already knowing the answer, "That was your father?"

Rex nodded. "Back when I was still at home, my father and mother mingled with owners and CEOs of major corporations on Oahu. Either they went to the same galas, state functions, or charity golf tournaments. My father spent time with Marcus Holte. I know this, not because he told me, but because he and Holte would show up on the news shaking hands over some deal or the opening of a new building. They played on the same team in a couple of the golf tournaments and had lunch with foreign dignitaries and politicians."

"You think your father might have inside information on Holte and what's happening with his shipments?"

Rex shrugged. "I figured it didn't hurt to ask."

"And what did your father say?"

"To be careful. Billionaires like Marcus Holte are untouchable." A frown pulled Rex's brow low on his forehead. "When I asked him what he meant by untouchable, he said, 'Think about it.'"

Kimo shook her head. "Does he mean they can get away with murder, and no one will do anything about it?"

"He didn't specify." Rex picked up his cell phone, selected a name and placed another call. This time, he put the call on speaker.

After one ring, Swede answered, "Rex, I was about to call you."

"Talk to me," Rex said.

"I looked up a fishing boat big enough to handle the container that was in Lanai's harbor at the same time as Holte's ship. It was in for maintenance and left within twenty-four hours. A large yacht came into the harbor shortly after the Holte ship arrived. It was flying a Panamanian flag. The type of yacht indicated it was also big enough to carry a twenty-foot container and could be rigged with a boom big enough to haul out of the water a large motorboat weighing about the same as your container. I'm still digging through corporate ownership and foreign-based LLCs to find the real owner. So, nothing specific, but a lead I'm chasing. What do you have?"

"I need you to dig into Marcus Holte. I had word from my father, James Johnson of JJ Enterprises, that I needed to beware of Holte. He said that he's untouchable."

"What did he mean by untouchable?" Swede asked.

"He didn't say." Rex met Kimo's eyes. "Kimo and I are betting he's not running a squeaky-clean operation. We think he might have enough money or influence to sway US and possibly international authorities to look the other way."

"I've been looking at his company and can't find anything that jumps out," Swede said.

"Then look at who he hangs out with," Rex said. "My father used to run in his circles. I'm thinking he still does and doesn't want to say anything."

"On it," Swede said. "You're on your way to your dive?"

"We are," Rex said.

"Good luck. I hope you find Kimo's camera. The authorities need that evidence to bring justice to the victims in that container. Out here."

Rex ended the call, set the phone in the cupholder and stared straight ahead, his jaw tight, his hands gripping the steering wheel so tightly his knuckles turned white.

Kimo reached out and touched his arm. "Are you as frustrated as I am?"

He nodded and flexed his fingers, letting blood flow into them. "I feel like we're on the edge of knowing something critical to solving this case."

"Me, too," she said. "It's like having a word on the tip of your tongue, but you can't spit it out."

"If only that word was the answer to all our questions." Rex continued driving, his focus on the road and, maybe, the situation. After a while, he turned to her. "I'm sorry."

Kimo looked at him. "For what?"

"That my father wasn't more forthcoming. I feel like he knows something that would help us with this situation. By holding back, it keeps you and Alana in danger." He banged his palm against the steering wheel. "It's just like him to protect his business associates and not come through for his family. Not that I'm a part of his family anymore. I'm actually shocked he spoke to me at all."

"Maybe he regrets having cut you off. Are you his only living relative?"

Rex nodded.

"He's older now. He might want to reconcile and rebuild your relationship."

"He can go to hell before I do that. He wasn't there for my mother. The only time he was there for me was to force his legacy on me, grooming me to join him in his business. Not that he cared about his son working with him so much as molding me to his specifications to be like him."

"How did you know?"

Rex snorted. "I heard him say he couldn't get enough employees who could think like him. He said, verbatim, 'I'll make sure you know how to run this business exactly as I would. No bellyaching. No going against my orders. You'll do precisely what I say. Won't you, boy?'"

Kimo stared at him in shock. "He said that?"

"He did," Rex said. "When my mother suggested I might want to choose a different career, he yelled at her that he wouldn't let his son bail on him. Why else would he have let her have a kid in the first place?"

"Ouch." Kimo winced. "That had to hurt her and you. How old were you when he said that?"

"Twelve." His face was grim as he drove into Lahaina, checking the rearview mirror often.

Kimo's heart ached for the twelve-year-old version of Rex. What a different childhood from hers, which had been filled with love and encouragement to explore her passions.

When they arrived at the marina, Rex parked in the parking lot, backing into the space. He jumped out, gathered his snorkel and mask and put on his sunglasses.

By the time he rounded the front of the truck, Kimo was pushing her door open.

He reached up, captured her waist in his hands

and swung her to the ground. His hands remained on her waist as he stared down into her eyes. "Anyone tell you your eyes are like dark, mysterious pools a person could fall into?"

She laughed. "No."

"Someone should." He smiled and tugged her hat down over her eyes. "Ready to go for our private snorkeling adventure?"

Kimo shoved her hat up in time to catch Rex winking at her. Her heart warmed at his playfulness in the face of so much danger. He'd just told her the story of his tragic family life and was trying to lighten her mood.

He took her sunglasses off her hat, where she'd rested them and placed them on her face. Then he caught her hand in his and walked her toward the marina.

Kimo guided him to Leilani's slips, where she kept her tour boats.

Leilani, wearing a polo shirt with her company logo embroidered across the top of her left breast, greeted them near the gangway. "Welcome to Windsong Tours, Mr. and Mrs. Lovejoy. I'm Leilani Kealoha, your tour guide. Please, come aboard. We're waiting on two more customers, and we'll be on our way for a fabulous evening of snorkeling."

Kimo grinned and joined the farce in case anyone in adjoining slips or on the dock was listening. "We've been looking forward to this since we arrived in Maui, haven't we, Snookums?" She leaned back into Rex and cupped his cheek in her palm. "I can't wait to see the little fishes, can you?"

He captured her hand in his and pressed a kiss to her knuckles. "Been counting the seconds, Doodlebug. Maybe we'll even see a turtle." His lips twitched as he looked toward Leilani. "Think we'll see a turtle, Ms. Kealoha?"

Leilani cocked an eyebrow at Rex. "We might." She waved a hand toward the gangway. "Please come aboard and make yourself comfortable."

Kimo crossed first, followed by Rex.

Angel waved from where he was arranging life vests, snorkels and masks. He waved at Kimo and Rex. "Aloha. I'm your deckhand, Angelo."

"Aloha, Angelo," Kimo responded.

Rex raised a hand at his teammate. "Angelo, where do we need to sit?"

Angel waved toward the benches lining each side of the interior. "Anywhere you like."

Rex and Kimo sat on the starboard bench.

A moment later, two men showed up, wearing swim trunks and Hawaiian shirts that didn't scream with their colors; they only chirped a little. They carried large gear bags and wore sunglasses and ball caps.

Kimo recognized Kiana's guy, Devlin Mulhaney, but not the other man with him. She assumed it was Teller Osgood, sent from the Big Island by his boss,

Jace Hawkins. She breathed a sigh of relief, knowing these men would provide cover on the boat while she, Angel, Leilani and Rex were diving.

The men boarded and found a seat on the opposite bench from Rex and Kimo.

Leilani unhooked the line from the cleat on the dock and tossed the line into the boat.

Angel grabbed it, wrapped it, lifted the lid of a box and laid it inside.

Leilani stepped aboard and drew in the gangway, stowing it on the side of the craft. She straightened and smiled. "We had an entire family cancel because they all came down with something. So, this is all of us. Sit back and relax as we take you on an adventure you won't soon forget." Her gaze swept the dock. "If you're ready, we'll get going. Angelo will give you the safety briefing on the way out of the marina." She strode through the boat to the helm and started the engine.

Soon, they were on their way out of the marina with Angel reciting the safety briefing until they were well out of earshot of anyone at the marina.

Once they were in open water, Leilani cranked up the speed and drove the boat along the west side of the island, heading for Maalaea Bay.

As soon as they were reasonably out of sight of land, Devlin and Teller opened their gear bags and extracted a rifle and handgun, along with extra magazines full of bullets.

Kimo's blood chilled, not so much at the weapons but at the fact that they might have to use them. What was the world coming to?

Rex reached for her hand and gave it a gentle squeeze. "They'll have our backs."

Kimo nodded.

Angel came through the cabin to hand Rex and Kimo wetsuits. A full-length one for Kimo to protect her injured leg and a shorter one for Rex. He grabbed one for himself, stripped out of his Windsong Tours polo shirt and slipped into the wetsuit. Then he took the helm while Leilani put on her gear.

Kimo shrugged out of her beach cover-up and stepped into the wetsuit. When she fumbled to find the armholes, Rex was there to help her. Once she was in it, he drew the zipper up the front, his knuckles skimming across her breasts.

Her breath caught and held as she raised her gaze to his. He stared down into her eyes for a long moment. "Everything's going to be all right," he said softly.

Kimo nodded, too flustered by how close he was and how much closer she wanted him to be.

He stepped back, took off his shirt and reached for his wetsuit.

She couldn't help herself. Kimo feasted her eyes on the man's broad, tanned chest, narrow waist and those loud, crazy-colored swim shorts.

"Good to see you're getting some use out of your

Ugly Hawaiian Outfit winner," Devlin said. "It's good that you'll be wearing a wetsuit over those trunks so that you don't scare the fish."

Rex's lips twisted. "Bite me." He dragged the wetsuit up his legs and zipped it before Kimo could offer to return the favor.

Leilani handed flippers to all four divers, then a mask and snorkel to Kimo.

Rex held his up. "Got my own."

Leilani nodded and checked the BCDs, regulators and tanks once more before taking the helm again.

Devlin rose to stand beside her as she showed him how to operate the tour boat. After a few moments, Dev took the helm while Leilani pointed ahead to the island, telling him what to look for and places he could pull into should he have to drive the tour boat.

Kimo hoped they wouldn't come to that. She wanted to get there, find the camera and get back before another boat full of gunmen showed up to cause trouble.

Devlin pulled a small buoy out of his bag and set it on the deck.

Angel and Rex moved to sit beside Devlin to adjust their dive watches and add preset messages.

Kimo watched with envy. She'd always wanted subwave sonar capabilities but had chosen to spend her profits on additional photography equipment and software first. She leaned forward, watching them adjust the buoy and their watches, eager to learn more.

"We already have *Are you okay?*," Devlin said. "And *Surface now*. What else should we add?"

"Low on air," Rex said.

"We don't know what we'll find down there," Kimo said. "How about *Incoming bogey?*"

Rex smiled at her. "That could mean anything dangerous—animal or human."

"Good," Dev said and keyed in the words.

"And how about *Need help?*" Angel added.

"Got it." Dev keyed in the message and tested them out on Angel's and Rex's watches, using the onboard monitoring device. "Now you two send a message to each other."

Angel sent one to Rex. Rex gave him a thumbs-up and sent a message to Angel.

Angel nodded. "Works."

"We need to be vigilant out there. These people aren't playing around," Rex said. "They don't want what's on that camera to get out, and they probably don't want anyone who has seen what was in that shipping container to live to tell about it."

"That would be Kimo and Alana," Angel said.

Rex moved to sit beside her. "We need to stay together. No more than three feet apart."

Kimo's brow furrowed. "We'll be bumping into each other."

"Better to bump into each other than to lose each other," he said softly.

"I'll be the same with Leilani," Dev grinned as Leilani chose that moment to glance back at them and cock a questioning eyebrow.

"Don't worry, babe. I've got you covered," Dev called out over the engine noise.

Leilani and Kimo had spent many hours together diving around Maui and the other islands. Kimo trusted her abilities. Angel, an ex-Navy SEAL, as well as Rex, had trained extensively in scuba diving. They had the right team.

"We'll start at the coordinates where we found the shipping container," Kimo said, "and then move toward the reef. We were on our way back to the dive boat when the other craft arrived and ran over Alana and then dragged her onboard. I headed for the reef when they came after me. I was close to the reef when bullets hit my scuba tank and grazed by leg."

Rex reached for Kimo's hand and held it as she continued.

Kimo liked how he made her feel safe. She drew in a breath and continued. "I dropped the BCD with the tank. I think that's when I dropped my camera, too, because I don't remember having it with me as I surfaced and hid among the rocks. If we can find the BCD and tank, the camera should be nearby."

"Since you were close to the reef, we'll spread out in pairs and swim in that direction," Rex said.

"And if we don't find it by the time we reach the reef?" Angel asked.

"We move along the base of the reef in opposite directions from there," Kimo said. "It has to be there." They had to find it. For Alana.

As they neared Maalaea Bay, Kimo stared out at the water and the sun that was moving closer to meet it. "We have about two hours before sunset. It will be easier to search while we have light than in the dark."

"So, let's make the best of daylight," Rex said.

Leilani slowed the tour boat, bringing it to a halt at the coordinates Kimo had given her.

Kimo stowed her cell phone in the console near the helm, removed the floppy hat and unwound her long, thick braid, letting it fall down her back. She fit her mask and snorkel over her head and reached for a BCD-tank combination.

Rex took it from her hands. "Let me."

Used to suiting up herself, Kimo's brow dipped momentarily.

"If it makes you feel better, you can help me next," he said with a smile.

"Deal." She turned and slipped her arms into the harness.

Rex settled the equipment on her shoulders, his hands lingering to adjust the fit. He turned her gently and buckled the straps in front.

While his focus was on the buckles, she studied his face. A five o'clock shadow spread across his chin, cheeks, and neck, but he'd taken time to shave his upper lip. Smart. The mask would fit better that way.

The stubble on his chin tempted her. She fought the urge to reach out and run her fingers across it to test its stiffness. She wondered how it would feel if he trailed kisses down her neck and across her breasts.

Rex was so close that she could easily fall against him and blame it on the waves rocking the boat.

His gray-eyed gaze rose to meet hers, a smile curving just the corners of his lips.

Could he read her thoughts? Heat bloomed in her chest, spreading upward into her cheeks.

A wave chose that moment to tilt the boat sharply.

Rex gripped the straps of her BCD, bringing her closer. Before she realized what was happening, he bent his head and brushed his lips across hers. That light touch was enough to spark a flame that rushed through her system like an out-of-control wildfire, burning a path through her and culminating at her core.

As quickly as it happened, it ended when Rex released her BCD and reached for another set. He held it out to her with a smile. "You turn."

She took the BCD and tank into shaking hands, her mind in turmoil, her thoughts ping-ponging like a pinball being batted back and forth. He turned his back to her, giving her a moment to pull herself together.

Rex slid his arms through the BCD harness and let her adjust it on his shoulders. When he turned, Kimo focused on the buckles, unable to meet his gaze, afraid he would see her feelings mirrored in her eyes.

That little bit of a kiss had rocked her even more than the waves tossing the tour boat.

What did it mean?

When her fingers fumbled with the buckles, Rex raised his hand to capture hers. "Hey. I'm sorry if I rattled you," he whispered. "I shouldn't have done that."

"Then why did you?" she asked, finally looking up into his eyes.

He shook his head. "I just...couldn't resist." His brow dipped. "I won't do it again," his tone deepened, "unless you want me to."

Kimo leaned toward him, caught in the moment, in the now stormy-gray of his eyes. "I—"

"We don't have much daylight left," Angel called out. "Are we ready?"

Kimo stepped back quickly and faced Angel and Leilani.

Leilani's brows were raised, her lips pressed together as if she wanted to say something but wouldn't.

Kimo ignored her knowing look, checked her gauges, grabbed her regulator and nodded. "Ready."

"Ready," Rex echoed.

Angel handed Kimo and Rex each a dive knife. "You might need these."

They secured the knives to their BCDs.

Typically, Kimo carried a knife, not only for protection, but to dig for interesting objects in the sand or on the reef. Having one now had an entirely different connotation, giving her a chill down her spine.

Devlin tied a line to the sonar buoy and dropped it into the water.

Kimo, Rex, Leilani and Angel moved to the back of the tour boat and sat to put on their fins and fit the regulators into their mouths.

With their masks fit over their faces, they dropped one by one into the water.

Teller stood on the deck, rifle in hand. "We'll cover the surface."

Devlin waved the sonar tracking device. "Check your watches."

Rex and Angel checked and gave Devlin a thumbs-up.

Kimo held up her hand with the okay sign. Once the other three repeated it, she pushed thoughts of Rex's kiss to the back of her mind and dove. She led the way to the bottom, where the shipping container had been. Her purpose for being there was to find her camera.

Alana's life depended on it.

CHAPTER 10

REX SWAM BESIDE KIMO, swinging his head back and
forth, keeping his eyes open and his senses on high
alert for any signs of danger from man or marine life.

As they neared the ocean floor, he looked around
for any sign of a shipping container or the people
who had died in it. As far as he could see, nothing
indicated that a twenty-foot shipping container had
rested in the sand. By now, the indentation would
have been smoothed over by current and wave
action.

Kimo pointed to Angel and Leilani, then to her
right toward the reef.

Leilani nodded, and the two swam away.

Instead of heading for the reef, Kimo hovered
over the sand. She pulled out her dive knife and dug
in several places.

Rex wasn't sure what she was doing. It wasn't like

the container could've sunk deep enough to be covered by the sand.

Rather than watch and wait, he joined her, digging his knife in a few inches and lifting sand.

A couple of minutes passed. Rex began to think they were wasting time they could be using to search for the BCD and camera. Ready to move on, he dug his knife in one last time. The tip of the knife struck something hard. When he lifted it, a metal crowbar came with the blade.

Kimo grabbed the crowbar and nodded. She motioned like she was jamming the crowbar into something to pry it open.

Rex understood what she was trying to say. This was the crowbar they'd used to open the container. Whether it could be used as evidence or not, she seemed happy to have found the tool. It was as if it proved she hadn't been hallucinating the existence of the shipping container.

She secured the crowbar to her BCD and motioned toward the reef.

Together, they swam toward the rocky outcropping.

Rex stayed with her, looking all around for the BCD she'd ditched during her escape from the shooters. A large school of shiny fish swam in front of them, their scales flashing like sequins in the sunlight.

They passed long stretches of sand with an occasional, isolated giant rock providing a home for coral and small, colorful fish. Rex tried to imagine how fast she'd had to have been swimming to evade the motorboat bearing down on her from above.

As she neared the reef, Kimo slowed and moved to the left. Rex stayed with her. Not exactly three feet away, but close enough to shield her if someone or something tried to get to her.

She swam several yards, moving in and out of the rocks along the edge.

A bright blue-and-green parrotfish swam around her as if warning her this was its feeding ground. When she swam past, it flipped its tail and went back to its territory.

Kimo moved on, continuing her search, widening the space between them and the other dive team.

A movement out of the corner of Rex's eyes drew his attention. He turned just as a turtle rose from the ocean floor and swam for the surface.

Caught in the moment, his gaze followed the turtle upward.

A strange humming sound made him look for the source.

Kimo searched the reef several feet ahead of him.

He hurried to close the distance, his gaze sweeping the water around them, looking for the hum that grew steadily louder.

Then he saw it.

A diver sped toward him using a propulsion vehicle. He held onto the device with one hand and aimed a speargun with the other.

Rex kicked hard to come up beside Kimo. He shoved her toward a crevice in between reef rocks as the approaching diver fired the speargun.

The spear sliced through the water, headed directly for Rex and Kimo.

He pushed her down and dove after her.

The spear crashed into the rock where a moment before Kimo had been.

Knowing the gun couldn't be reloaded very fast, Rex tapped his watch, sending the message *Need Help Now.* He didn't wait for a response. Instead, he swam up as the man with the propulsion vehicle passed over them, turned around and paused to reload.

Rex wasn't giving him a chance to shoot again. He swam, pushing as hard and fast as he could, and catching the attacker before he could fit the spear into the weapon. Rex grabbed the gun, yanked it from the man's hands and flung it away.

A knife flashed past Rex's face.

He ducked, grabbed his knife and thrust it toward the other man, slicing into his arm.

The man jerked backward, blood coloring the water around him.

When Rex shot a glance over his shoulder toward Kimo, his heart skipped a beat. She had come out of the rocks and was swimming toward him.

Behind her, another man approached with a

propulsion vehicle, aiming directly for her. Unlike his predecessor, he wasn't carrying a speargun, which was Kimo's saving grace.

Kimo must have heard the hum of the approaching propulsion vehicle. She turned in time to see the incoming threat and quickly retreated, ducking low behind the rocks, disappearing completely.

Rex kicked hard, swimming for her, angry at himself for ignoring his own rule to stay within three feet of her. He prayed he'd reach her before the man with the DPV.

His prayer wasn't answered.

Before he was within ten feet of Kimo, the man on the DPV reached her location first and slowed to a stop.

Kimo shot upward, slamming the crowbar into the man's gut.

The attacker spun away. He seemed to regroup and then renewed his attack, charging Kimo as she hovered over the reef, backpaddling desperately to swim back into the relative cover of the rocks while moving further away from the attacker and Rex.

The other diver went after Kimo, dropping behind the reef, out of Rex's sight.

Rex's heart sputtered, and he pushed harder. He cleared the rocks in time to see the man with his hands around Kimo's throat.

She kicked and swung her arms at the man, trying

to free herself from his grip. When her hand landed on his face mask, she grabbed it and yanked it off his face.

The attacker released one hand from Kimo's throat and reached for the mask in her hand.

She flung it into the rocks of the reef and used that moment to shove him backward into Rex.

Rex hooked the man's arm and swung him around and away from Kimo.

The aggressor came at Rex with his knife, swinging it wildly, his eyes squeezed tightly shut against the stinging saltwater.

Rex reached for the man's wrist and shoved it against a jagged rock. The fight moved as if in slow motion. Every shove sent his opponent in one direction and Rex in the opposite.

He had the advantage over the other guy because he didn't have his mask, and the saltwater was clearly causing him distress. Finally, the man touched the inflater assembly on his left shoulder, sending him toward the surface.

Rex's watch pinged from the guys on the surface with the message, *Incoming Bogey.* He glanced up to see the propeller and underside of a speeding boat whip past them.

When he looked toward Kimo, she was waving frantically and pointing behind him.

Before he could turn, someone rammed into him and pushed him away while tugging at the hose connecting his regulator to the tank. He clamped his teeth around the mouthpiece and held on.

Rex twisted, trying to spin and face the aggressor. When he did, the strain on his regulator hose snapped, and he sucked water in through his mouthpiece.

His hose had been cut.

Rex spat out the water and ruined regulator, held his breath and blocked a jab from a knife the guy held. He didn't have time to fight this guy. He needed to get to the surface and air. He let the diver come close, blocked his attempt to cut him and delivered his own knife into the man's midsection, sinking it deep.

The diver clutched his belly and kicked away. He swung the propulsion vehicle up from where a strap attached it to his BCD. Moments later, he blasted past them, leaving a trail of blood and bubbles.

His lungs burning for air, Rex started for the surface.

A hand on his arm stopped him. He turned to find Kimo beside him. She removed the regulator from her mouth and held it in front of his face.

He took it, sucked in a deep breath, let it out and took another. Panic abated, and he handed the regulator back to Kimo.

She put the regulator in her mouth and pointed to the surface.

He gave her the okay sign and grabbed her BCD,

bringing her chest to chest with him. He held on as they kicked their fins, rising no faster than the bubbles from the breaths they released.

They hadn't gone far when Rex realized all was not well at the surface.

That motorboat that had zoomed over their heads had turned around and slowed to a stop above them.

Rex and Kimo stopped their ascent and reversed course, sinking back among the reef rocks, continuing to share the air from her tank.

The people above hauled one of their divers aboard. The wounded diver who'd sped away on the DPV raced up to the boat. He, too, was dragged aboard.

About the time the boat finally sped away, Angel and Leilani converged on them.

Angel messaged Rex, *Are you all right?*

Rex gave him the hand signal for okay and rose with Kimo, buddy-breathing all the way to the surface.

Devlin and Teller brought the tour boat close enough to where they were, without risking running into the reef.

Waves splashed over them, the water rougher than when they'd started the dive. The sun hovered over the horizon, appearing to slowly melt into the ocean.

Devlin helped Leilani up onto the boat while Teller stood guard with a rifle.

Rex pulled himself out of the water and turned to help Kimo on board.

"Are you okay?" he asked, inspecting her neck. "Did he hurt you?"

Kimo shook her head. "He didn't have me long enough."

Rex didn't see any bruising. He relaxed a little. "You scared me."

She laughed. "You scared me, going after the man with the speargun."

"He missed the first time." Rex inhaled and let it out slowly. "He might not have missed a second time. I couldn't let him reload. But I left you, and I shouldn't have."

"You had to stop him—and you came back."

Once Angel was on the tour boat, they worked at stripping out of their BCDs, tanks and fins.

"I take it you ran into some trouble down there," Devlin said as he helped stow tanks.

"We did," Rex said.

"We had some excitement up here, as well," Teller said.

"A boat with a couple of men played chicken with us and then opened fire." Devlin grimaced. "I'm sorry, Leilani, but some of those bullets hit your boat."

"As long as you two are okay, we can fix the boat," Leilani said as she shrugged out of her BCD. "We just have to get it back to the marina before it takes on too much water."

"The camera?" Teller asked.

Kimo shook her head. "We didn't find it." She glanced toward Leilani, her lips pressing together.

Leilani shook her head. "We didn't see the camera or the ditched BCD and tank." She glanced toward the sunset. "We could go back down, but it's hard enough to search for them in the daylight. We can start again first thing in the morning."

Kimo faced the west where the sun had sunk below the horizon, leaving them in the gray haze of dusk. "That storm is supposed to hit us late tomorrow night."

"Already the ocean is stirring," Angel said. "The waves are growing and will be worse tomorrow. Will it be too dangerous to dive?"

"Dangerous or not," Kimo squared her shoulders, "I have to find that camera."

"I'll be out here at first daylight," Leilani promised.

Angel frowned his displeasure. "I'll be with you."

"As will I," Kimo said.

Rex wasn't any happier than Angel about the rough seas and the possibility of running into more trouble from whoever had come at them that day. Kimo wouldn't be deterred. If Kimo was going down again...

Rex met Kimo's gaze. "I'll be here, too."

Leilani took over the helm and drove the tour boat north toward Lahaina.

Angel held up his cell phone. "I'll update Hawk on how it went."

Rex nodded and helped Kimo out of her wetsuit, peeling it down her body and exposing her bright red bikini. His lips twitched at the cheerful color and style that seemed so incongruous with the danger they'd just faced.

Then again, she was an underwater photographer, not a military-trained operator. She shouldn't have to be worried about attacks from humans. Nor should she have found a container full of dead people.

Kimo slipped her cover-up over her shoulders, twisted her damp braid around the crown of her head and fit the floppy hat over it.

Rex was amazed at the transformation from a serious diver who had just been attacked underwater to vacationing Mrs. Lovejoy. She seemed so calm and collected. Her Hawaiian heritage gave her an exotic beauty unlike any he'd ever encountered. He found it harder and harder to pull back and remind himself she was the client. He was the protector.

Rex moved away in an attempt to put distance between himself and Kimo. He stripped off his wetsuit, pulled on the loud Hawaiian shirt and grabbed his cell phone from where he'd stowed it near the helm.

As they neared the marina, Leilani reduced their speed to comply with the no-wake zone and maneuvered the tour boat into its slip. Angel leaped out onto the dock and secured the lines.

Rex's phone pinged with an incoming text from his father. He frowned down at the message.

JJohnson: If you want to talk to Holte, meet me at Maalaea Small Boat Harbor at 9:00 pm tonight. Dress code formal attire. Come alone

Rex: ?

JJohnson: No questions. Just be there

He glanced up, his gaze meeting Kimo's concerned one.

"What's wrong?" she asked.

"I'm not sure." He showed the message to Kimo.

Teller and Devlin leaned close to read the message as well.

Leilani cut the engine and came to stand close to Kimo, looking over her shoulder.

"Do you think he's set up a meeting between you and Holte?" Kimo asked.

"Why formal attire?" Devlin shook his head. "Sounds like he's taking you to an event."

Angel joined them. "On a marina?"

"Some luxury yacht owners have parties on board their big yachts docked at the marinas," Leilani said. "He could be taking you to a party your father and Holte have been invited to."

Rex nodded. That sounded right. "Does Holte have a yacht large enough to accommodate a black-tie event?"

"Ask Swede," Angel said.

Rex texted Swede, giving him a screenshot of the message his father had sent.

Rex: Does Holte have a yacht moored at Maalaea Small Boat Harbor?

Swede: I'll get back to you

While they waited for Swede's response, they gathered tanks and BCDs and carried them to Leilani's dive and snorkeling shop. They spent the next thirty minutes preparing for the next day's dive since they would be leaving before dawn to get to Maalaea Bay at first light. By the time they had filled tanks and replaced the damaged regulator, seven o'clock was approaching.

If he was to meet his father at nine, Rex needed to get to his apartment, shower and change.

"Do you have formal wear?" Kimo asked.

He nodded. "I have the black suit I wore to my buddy's funeral. Though I haven't decided if I'll go."

"Why not?" Kimo asked. "It might be our only chance to talk to Holte."

He grasped her hands in his. "I can't take you with me."

"Of course, you can't." Kimo shook her head. "Your father said you had to come alone."

"If you're not with me, I can't protect you."

Leilani walked by at that moment. "That's not an issue. Angel and I will stay with Kimo until you return."

Rex didn't like leaving Kimo for even a minute. It was more than just protecting her. He stared down into her eyes. He wasn't sure what more it was, but it definitely made him leery about leaving her. "You're my responsibility," he said.

Kimo laid a hand on his chest. "You have to do it. Any information about that container has to lead to finding Alana. If Holte has any information, you have to get it out of him. You have to meet with him." She nodded toward Angel. "Do you trust your teammates?"

"With my life," Rex said.

"Then you can trust them with mine." Kimo squared her shoulders. "It's settled. You're going."

His lips curled up on the corners. "Yes, ma'am."

Rex's cell phone chirped with an incoming call. Swede's name flashed on the screen. Rex answered the call and put it on speaker. "Swede, you're on speaker."

"Good. I added Hawk to the conversation," Swede said.

"Hey, guys. I gave Swede the rundown on what happened with your dive."

"Sorry to hear you met with resistance and didn't find the camera," Swede said.

"We'll try again in the morning," Rex said.

"I've been watching the reports on the storm headed your way," Swede said. "It doesn't look good."

"It shouldn't hit until later tomorrow night," Rex

said. "What did you find out about Holte? Does he have a yacht?"

"Yes, Holte owns a yacht, but it's moored in California. There are several other yachts moored at the Maalaea Small Boat Harbor, but only one, the Dancing Lolita, is large enough to handle a formal party of billionaires, and it only docked there this morning to restock. I had to dig through several layers of corporations and LLCs to find the owner— a Lucien Vaughan."

"Hey, Swede, Angel here," Angel said. "They must be hustling to put on a party for the rich and famous."

"Money moves things along," Swede said. "I did a search on Lucien Vaughan and found him all over the world with billionaires, foreign dignitaries and US politicians. He moves in high circles and seems to attract people with money. He's known for attending as well as throwing lavish parties at his homes in California, New York City, Paris and on his yacht."

Rex sighed. "Sounds like Vaughan's yacht will be my destination tonight." He thought he'd left the world of high rollers behind with his father. He hadn't missed the ostentatious gatherings.

As a child, he hadn't had to attend many. At those events, his parents had dressed him in a suit, his father threatening severe punishment if he embarrassed him in any way. Yeah, he'd happily left that world behind for a real life with men he could respect for their actions, not for the size of their bank accounts.

His gaze went to Kimo.

She reached for his hand. "For Alana," she whispered. "Thank you."

He held onto her hand as he faced Angel and Leilani. "I'd prefer you stay with Kimo at my place. I have to go there to change and get ready, and I'll come back there after the meeting with Holte."

Angel nodded. "We'll stay with Kimo there."

"Do you need us there as well?" Devlin asked.

Rex shook his head. "I have a security system. As long as Angel and Leilani are there with Kimo, I think she'll be all right."

"Then we'll be on our way." Devlin tipped his head toward Teller. "Ready?"

Teller nodded. "If you need us, we'll be on alert for the call."

"Thank you," Kimo said then turned to Rex. "We'd better get going, or you'll be late."

Rex slipped an arm around Kimo's waist and walked her to his truck. Once they were settled inside, he drove out of the parking lot, heading for his apartment on the other side of the island.

Angel and Leilani followed in Angel's vehicle.

Rex was glad to have Kimo to himself for the drive. "Are you okay?" he asked.

She nodded. "I am. But I'm worried."

"About?'

"You," she said softly.

He glanced her way. "I'll be fine. Only, I don't like leaving you."

She laughed. "I'll have protection. What will you have?"

"My father is meeting me. Though we haven't been on speaking terms since my mother's death, I can't believe he'd lead me into a death trap."

Kimo's eyebrows rose. "Has he tried to contact you in all that time?"

Rex frowned. "No. He clearly disowned me when I joined the Army."

"Then why do you any favors now?" she asked.

The same thoughts had crossed Rex's mind. "Guilt?" Even as he said it, he doubted the idea.

Kimo snorted. "Based on all you've told me, the man has no compassion or possibly no moral compass—much like the people who sank the shipping container with people inside it."

"My father is giving me the chance to speak with Holte. I'm taking the chance." He reached for her hand. "If we don't find that camera, we have no leverage. We have to do whatever we can to help our friend."

Kimo's fingers tightened around his. "In the short amount of time we've been together, I feel like we've known each other for a lifetime. I'd hate for anything to happen to you. I kind of like having you around."

Rex's heart squeezed hard in his chest. "I kind of

like being around." He lifted his chin. "I'll be careful. As much as I trust Angel to protect you, I'd rather be the one."

Kimo nodded and brought his hands to her lips, pressing a soft kiss to the backs of his knuckles.

Rex held onto her words and the feeling of her lips against his skin as he drove the rest of the way to his apartment.

He didn't like that murderers had drowned people in a shipping container. He was furious that the same murderers held Kimo's friend hostage. He didn't like that Kimo was in danger. If he had to walk into a lion's den, he would for them.

For her.

CHAPTER 11

WHILE KIMO PACED outside Rex's room, Angel and Leilani raided the kitchen.

"Looks like we have a choice between leftover pizza, moldy cheese, or eggs," Leilani said. "Choose your poison."

"I'm not hungry." Kimo continued pacing.

Leilani pulled plates from a cabinet and set Angel to work microwaving pizza. She emerged from the kitchen and stood close to Kimo's path. "He's going to be all right."

Kimo stopped. "How do you know? He doesn't even know where exactly he's going. His father, whom he hasn't spoken with for over a decade, says to meet him at a marina, no questions. Who does that?"

Leilani shrugged. "I don't like that part either, but Rex is trained in special operations."

"The difference between his experience and what's happening now is that he knew who the enemy was." Kimo threw up her hands. "We don't know who's behind what's going on."

Angel came out of the kitchen, carrying two plates piled with pizza slices. "The thing about knowing who the enemy was isn't true. There were many operations we went into where we didn't know who was friend and who was foe." He laid the plates on the dinette table. "We relied on quick reflexes and instinct to get out of tight situations or to protect our brothers in arms. Rex has good instincts and the added experience of growing up around the rich and morally challenged. He's not going in completely blind."

Kimo tipped back her head and closed her eyes in an attempt to calm her wildly beating heart. "I hear you."

She opened her eyes and gave her friends a weak smile. "Rex has combat training and experience working with a team. I worry that he's going alone. No one will have his six like he's had mine."

"I don't like that either," Angel said. "But Rex is a smart guy."

"Perfect timing for my entrance," a deep voice sounded behind Kimo.

Kimo turned, and her breath lodged in her lungs.

Rex stepped out of his bedroom, clean-shaven, his

hair slicked back, the black, tailored suit making his gray eyes even darker.

When he smiled at her, he took her breath away. "Is this okay?"

Dumbstruck, all Kimo could do was nod.

Leilani let out a low whistle. "Wow," she said. "You clean up nicely."

"Thanks," he responded without taking his gaze away from Kimo. "Think my father would approve?"

Kimo blinked. "Who cares what he thinks? You look…"

"Like James Bond." Angel walked around Rex with a huge grin on his face.

"Sexy as hell." Leilani slid an arm around Kimo. "Wouldn't you agree?"

Kimo nodded automatically. The man was hot anyway. In a form-fitting black suit, he made her weak in the knees.

Rex glanced at his watch. "I have a GPS tracker in my pocket. Angel, add it to your cell phone finder. That way you can track where I'm going."

Kimo swallowed hard at the lump forming in her throat. "In case they kidnap you?" She stepped close to him and laid a hand on his chest. "I don't feel at all good about this. Maybe you shouldn't go."

He laid his hand over hers and stared down into her eyes. "I have to. It's my father. He knows Holte. If we have a fraction of a chance to learn the whereabouts of Alana, I have to take that chance."

Rex lifted her hand to his lips and pressed a kiss to her palm. "I'll be okay."

"Promise?" Kimo whispered. "I kind of like having you around."

He nodded. "I'm not any happier about leaving you." With a nod toward Angel, he continued, "Angel and Leilani will be with you. I'll be back as soon as possible."

Angel added the tracking device to his cell phone finder, shook Rex's hand and then pulled him into a hug. "Don't do anything I wouldn't do."

Rex laughed. "That leaves the field wide open."

"Okay," Angel's lips twisted. "Just remember this is recon. Gather information and get out of there."

"Will do." Rex reached for Kimo's hand. "Walk me to the door?"

Kimo laid her hand in his and let him pull her close. As she walked toward the apartment exit, she leaned into him, soaking up his strength and the scent of his cologne.

He stopped short of the door and turned to face her. "Kimo, we've only been together a short period of time, but I've never felt as close to any woman as I do to you. You're strong, intelligent, feisty, and you care about your friends and people you don't even know." His voice lowered to where only she could hear. "More than anything, I want to be with you, to keep you safe, to hold you and to—"

Her heart pounding hard in her chest, Kimo flung her arms around his neck, leaned up on her toes and said, "Shut up and kiss me already."

His lips curled as his arms came up around her, pulling her body up against his. He claimed her mouth with his in a mind-blowing, pulse-pounding kiss that rocked her world.

She opened to him. Their tongues met and swept together in a wave of passion Kimo had never experienced.

When he set her back on her feet, she swayed, her hands sinking to his chest, her gaze rising to meet his. "Be careful."

He nodded, kissed the tip of her nose and disappeared through the door, closing it softly between them.

All the air left Kimo's lungs like a deflating balloon as she reached out to twist the deadbolt. She rested her head against the cool panel. Finally, she remembered to breathe, drew in a breath and let it out slowly.

A hand on her back made her turn, and she was drawn into Leilani's arms.

"He'll be back," she murmured, holding Kimo close.

"If it makes you feel any better," Angel said from across the room, "Devlin and Teller are headed to Maalaea Small Boat Harbor now. They'll infiltrate silently and remain hidden, watching Rex's every move. They'll be there if he gets in trouble."

Kimo hugged Leilani once and stepped back in relief. "That does make me feel marginally better. As long as they don't take him away on a boat, somewhere they can't get to him like Alana."

"Hopefully, that won't happen," Angel said. "In the meantime, we wait and hope Rex comes back with something we can use to locate Alana."

"Hey, come sit." Leilani walked with Kim to the sofa and sat down beside her. "Based on that kiss, I'd say you really like the guy."

Kimo nodded and frowned, looking into her friend's eyes. "Is it too soon? Battle-forged attraction? Crazy? Real?" She twisted her hands together in her lap.

Leilani laughed. "All the above. Sometimes, it's a case of when you know, you know." She patted Kimo's hands and squeezed them gently. "We never know how long we have in our lives. I learned that during the Lahaina fires." Her gaze shifted to Angel eating pizza at the table. "You have to grab for happiness whenever and wherever you find it."

"I'm almost thirty years old. I've dated men, but I've never felt this before. It's so achingly beautiful it's almost painful."

Leilani gathered Kimo's hands in hers and gave her a watery smile. "Honey, if you're not in love already, you're well on your way there."

"What if he doesn't feel the same?" Kimo whispered.

From across the room, Angel answered, "Trust me, I've never seen Rex say so many words to a woman before. He might not realize it yet, but he's absolutely, no-going-back smitten."

Kimo shook her head. Insta-love didn't exist. What she was feeling had to be a product of living through danger together. When the danger was over, would they have anything in common? Would there be enough to forge a lasting relationship?

She hoped with all her heart that they lived long enough to find out.

REX DROVE across the island to Maalaea Bay, his thoughts on the meeting with his father warring with the kiss he'd shared with Kimo before he'd left.

He'd gone into many dangerous situations free of distraction from what he was leaving behind, able to commit his entire focus on the mission ahead and his teammates with him.

Now, his thoughts were on getting through the meeting with Holte, if it truly happened, and getting back to Kimo.

The whole leaving a loved one behind was messing with his mind, his concentration and... his body. His pulse raced, and his heartbeat alternated between pounding and fluttering.

Who was he?

One passionate kiss shouldn't have him acting like a teenager after his first date with a gorgeous girl. He wanted to immediately see her again. The attraction was so strong, all he could think about was taking her to the next level as soon as possible.

Before he realized it, he was pulling off the highway into the Maalaea Small Boat Harbor.

Mission on. Time to bring his focus back to his purpose for being there, dressed in a suit with a tie already choking him. Not because it was tight, but because he hated wearing them.

He drove his truck into the parking lot ten minutes before nine o'clock, backed into a space and glanced around at the other vehicles parked there. Several limousines were lined up side by side, also backed into their spaces, their drivers sitting behind the wheels. His truck stood out among the gleaming black vehicles. He shrugged and waited, glancing down the long stretch of boat slips filled with crafts of different types and lengths. His gaze came to rest on the largest yacht moored near the middle of the paved dock, lights glaring, people already milling about on board.

A black limousine rolled into view in front of the slip with the brightly lit yacht. A man emerged alone.

Rex's chest tightened. From a distance, he couldn't mistake the way the man stood, straight as an arrow, his chin raised, hand tucked into the lapel of his suit. Aside from his hair having turned gray, he was the same. James Johnson. Rex's father.

Rex drew in a breath, reminded himself that his father had no hold over him and dropped down from his truck.

Music drifted in the air, growing louder as Rex strode the length of the dock, passing cars parked in front of slips with smaller yachts and sailboats. His gaze zeroed in on the man he'd sworn he'd never speak to again.

So much for swearing.

Necessity drove him forward. A woman's life hung in the balance.

His gaze swept over the yacht, noting the helipad on the roof and a crane, draped in twinkle lights, perched over the wide deck now filled with guests. The name emblazoned in gold lettering across the back proclaimed the yacht Dancing Lolita—Lucien Vaughan's yacht. A matching, smaller motorboat occupied the slip beside the yacht with the name La Petite Lolita written across its stern.

His father approached the gangway.

Four security guards stood, two each, on either side of the slip, eyes narrowed, armed and alert for any trouble.

A beautiful young blonde, dressed in a black, form-hugging gown, stood at the gangway, a leather-bound notebook in her hand.

James Johnson was speaking with her as Rex approached.

The woman nodded, touched a hand to her ear and spoke into a microphone curving around her cheek. After a moment, she nodded and smiled as Rex came to a stop beside his father. "I take it this is your son, Mr. Johnson? He looks like you."

His father turned, his gray eyes meeting Rex's for the first time in thirteen years. "Yes, this is James Rex Johnson the second," he said, his tone flat and emotionless. "My son."

Rex fought the urge to correct the man. He hadn't been addressed by his full name since he'd lived with his parents, and only when he'd been in trouble for some minor infraction.

"My apologies, Mr. Johnson," the hostess said to Rex. "I'll need to see a form of identification."

Rex pulled his wallet from the inside pocket of his jacket and handed the woman his driver's license.

She made a note in her notebook, handed the license back to Rex, then smiled and waved a hand toward the gangway. "Welcome aboard the Dancing Lolita."

Rex followed his father up the gangway onto the deck, where men in tailored suits and diamond cufflinks, and women in flashy designer gowns, dripping with expensive jewelry, milled about, drinking champagne from crystal glasses.

The tie around Rex's neck seemed to tighten. He'd

gladly left this world behind. He'd be happy to leave it again. First, he had to find Holte and learn more about his shipping business, specifically, about a missing container, the bodies inside it and the people who'd reclaimed them.

How he'd address those questions was still mulling around in his head. He couldn't just ask them outright, especially if Holte knew all about them and had a lot to hide.

His father led him through the throng of billionaires and a scattering of celebrities, including a race car driver, an A-list actor and his wife and several Hawaiian politicians Rex recognized from the local news.

His father headed for the bar and ordered an Old Fashioned. He didn't ask Rex what he wanted to drink.

Rex moved to the second bartender and ordered a whiskey neat.

Once they both had their drinks, his father turned toward the crowd of people, took a sip of his Old Fashioned and asked, "Do you know who's throwing this party?"

Rex nodded. "Lucien Vaughan."

"Vaughan has worldwide influence. If you want to increase your global presence, talk to Lucien. If you want to know where to invest in the next potential gold rush of an economy, Lucien's your guy. Everyone on board tonight owes significant portions of their wealth to the information Lucien provides."

"What do they give him in return?" Rex asked.

His father's eyes narrowed. "You don't ask."

"Meaning, *you* don't ask."

His father's brow dropped low. "You don't rock the boat, unless yours capsizes."

"So, he's got dirt on all these people and holds it over their heads and bank accounts." He didn't ask. It was a statement.

A young woman dressed in a strapless, short and tight black-and-white uniform stopped in front of them with a tray of crystal glasses full of champagne. With a decidedly Slavic accent, she asked, "*Șampanie?*" As soon as the word was out, she covered her mouth, and her cheeks flushed red. She glanced around quickly and said, "Pardon. I mean Champagne."

Rex studied her pretty face, noting how smooth and youthful it appeared. It was slightly rounded with no lines around the eyes. Either she had youthful genes, or she was very young.

He shook his head and held up his glass and responded, "*Nu, mulțumesc.*"

The girl's eyes widened, and her cheeks grew redder. She bobbed her head and hurried away in her short skirt and sheer, black tights.

"What are you doing?" his father hissed.

"Being polite," Rex said.

"Don't talk to the wait staff," his father said.

"Why?"

"Just don't." His father glanced around. "You wanted to talk to Holte, there he is." He motioned with his head. "The tall, heavyset man with gray hair and a mustache. He's standing with Lucien Vaughan and his partner, Chloé."

The man he indicated stood with another man and a dark-haired woman in a shimmering silver gown. The other man with salt-and-pepper hair had his back to Rex and his arm around the woman in the silver dress.

Another young woman, dressed in the black-and-white, skimpy uniform, approached Holte, Vaughan and Chloé with a tray of drinks. This girl also appeared to be very young, like the Romanian girl.

"If you still want to talk to Holte, you're on your own," his father said and walked away.

Rex stood for a moment, debating whether he should interrupt the two men or wait until he could get Holte alone. He set his glass on a nearby table, ready to charge in and get the interview over.

He hadn't taken two steps before the first waitress he'd encountered appeared in front of him with another tray, this one full of hors d'oeuvres. "Would you like?"

Rex shook his head, his attention on the men, not wanting to let them out of his sight.

"Please," she said and moved to block his view.

Rex shifted his gaze to the girl, his eyes narrowing. Curious. "*Câți ani ai?*" He asked how old she was.

She shot a glance over her shoulder and answered quietly, "*Paisprezece ani.*" Fourteen years old.

Rex's jaw tightened. Over her shoulder, the two men parted, Vaughan moving away with his partner, leaving Holte briefly alone.

"*Scuzați-mă,*" he said to the waitress and moved around her.

What the hell was a fourteen-year-old girl doing working on a yacht? Determined to accomplish his mission of cornering Holte for answers, he moved toward the man.

Holte waved a hand toward someone across the deck. Before he could cross to join that person, Rex stepped in front of the owner of Holte Maritime Group.

"Mr. Holte," Rex stuck out his hand. "Rex Johnson, pleasure to meet you."

Holte frowned but took Rex's hand. "Should I know you?"

"Yes, of course. I'm Rex Johnson of RJ Direct Source Imports, soon to be the leading importer of commodities from Asia. I'd hoped to speak with you about your company's capabilities and willingness to take on a rising star in import management."

Holte dropped Rex's hand. "This isn't the time or place to discuss business. Talk to my CEO during operational hours." He moved to go around Rex.

Rex lowered his voice. "Sir, I'd rather work directly with the man in charge." Taking a stab in the dark, he moved closer. "I understand you're the one who can transport specialized cargo. Cargo that needs special attention and handling."

Holte froze, his eyes narrowing. "We handle all types of cargo. Again, speak to my CEO for your specific needs."

"I was told you're the one I needed to speak with." Rex blocked the man in a corner of the deck. "I'm interested in transporting cargo that needs delicate handling. Rumor has it your ships have the capability I'm looking for and the access that can deliver my cargo safely. We're talking priceless commodities in small shipments."

"I don't know what you're talking about." He started to wave toward someone behind Rex.

"My concern is your ability to deliver the cargo." Rex stepped closer to Holte. "Rumor has it, you lost a small container recently, and the contents within were destroyed. I want to know what guarantees you can give me that won't happen to my shipments."

Holte's face paled. "We take pride in delivering all cargo without fail. However, we lose an occasional container due to circumstances out of our control."

"What circumstances?" Rex narrowed his eyes.

"Primarily weather," Holte responded.

"What else?"

"There are a number of other things that could

cause the loss of a container. I refuse to go into the details here." He shrugged. "The price you charge for your commodities should build in a potential loss factor. Now, if you'll excuse me, I have business with someone else." The shipping tycoon pushed past Rex.

Rex let him go without reminding the man he'd said this wasn't the place to discuss business. Based on his discomfort, Holte knew about the missing container.

After Holte disappeared into the interior of the yacht, Rex looked around for his father. He was nowhere to be found on the deck.

Having potentially scared Holte by mentioning the missing container, Rex felt he had nothing to lose by asking him more direct questions. He pushed through the glass door into the interior of the yacht. The room he stepped into was all white leather and gold accents. A large room spread out before him with a bar at the far end and a few people scattered around, seated in the plush leather sofas curving into intimate half-circles.

He didn't see Holte, Vaughan or his father. Rex ambled across the floor toward a door at the far side of the room, which led deeper into the yacht.

A man dressed in the same uniform as the men standing guard on the dock stepped in front of him. "This area is off limits to guests."

Rex held up his hands. "Sorry. I was just exploring. It's a beautiful boat. I'm thinking of getting one for myself."

The guard's face remained set. He didn't move from his position.

Rex walked away, heading for the bar where he ordered a whiskey neat. Once he had the drink in hand, he strode over to a window. He stared out at the other boats moored in the harbor while watching the room behind him in the window's reflection and the off-limits door in his peripheral vision.

Several minutes passed before the door opened.

Rex's father came out. The door closed behind him.

The man crossed to the bar and ordered whiskey. As soon as the bartender placed the glass in front of him, he tossed it back and asked for another.

When the second glass was placed in front of him, James Johnson lifted it and glanced around the room. When he spotted Rex, he moved in his direction.

Rex kept his gaze aimed toward the harbor while watching his father approach in the window's reflection.

When he came to a stop beside Rex, he quietly said, "You opened a can of worms."

Rex played dumb. "How so?"

"Whatever you said to Holte spooked him. He wanted to know everything about you." His father met his gaze in the reflection. "You told him you were a commodities importer?"

Rex shrugged. "Seemed a good idea at the time."

"What game are you playing, son?" his father demanded.

"The real question is what game is Holte playing?" He met his father's gaze and held it. "And maybe I should ask what part you have in it?"

His father's frown deepened into a scowl. "Who the hell are you to question my associations? You wanted nothing to do with my business thirteen years ago. Why are you interested now?"

"I never have and never will have any interest in your business." Rex lowered his voice to barely above a whisper, kept a poker face and added, "If your business deals in human trafficking, sex trafficking of underage females and murder, I'll do everything in my power to shut you and your friends down." He followed his words with a tight-lipped smile.

"You don't know who you're dealing with."

"I have a start with Holte and possibly you."

The door Rex had kept in his peripheral vision opened.

Holte walked out, followed by Lucien Vaughan. Vaughan had his hand on Holte's back. He said something only Holte could hear, patted him on the back and looked around the room.

His gaze landed on Rex and his father.

"Now, I'll bet Lucien Vaughan is another piece to the puzzle," Rex said. "Brace yourself. He's coming."

His father stiffened beside him.

"James," Lucien called out. "Where have you been hiding your son?"

James Johnson schooled his face and turned. "He's been busy in the Army."

"How is it this is the first time I've met him?"

Rex's father waved a hand between Lucien and Rex. "Lucien Vaughan, my son, Rex."

Lucien's brow rose. "The Army, you say?" He held out his hand to Rex. "Thank you for your service."

Rex gave a brief nod. "Nice yacht you have."

"Thanks. It was a gift from a Saudi prince a couple of years ago. They know how to outfit a yacht in luxury." He waved a hand around the room. "I've added a few things and changed a few to meet my needs."

"Was the crane on it or added?" Rex asked.

"I had it added last year," he said. "I like to carry my own tender boat."

"What is the weight capacity of the crane?" Rex asked.

"Approximately seventy thousand pounds," Vaughan said. "Give or take."

"With a crane like that, you could go into the salvage business and raise cargo from the ocean floor, couldn't you?" Rex knew he was pushing it.

Vaughan smiled. "I've considered it. I'm intrigued by the idea of discovering sunken treasure."

"Do you scuba dive?" Rex asked. "Would you participate in diving to find the sunken treasure?"

Vaughan shook his head. "Other than a little recreational diving, I'd leave the treasure hunting dives to the experts."

Rex glanced around the room. "I bet it takes a large crew to run a yacht this size. Do you have your own divers to maintain the hull?"

"Some members of my crew go under to scrape barnacles when necessary. I have the Lolita serviced twice a year to keep the hull clean and the engines in top shape."

"Have you ever had a diver injured while diving for you?" Rex asked.

The man had a poker face. The only indication that Rex might have struck a nerve was a slight tightening of Vaughan's jaw.

"Not once," Vaughan said. "Now we've had crew members slip and fall on a wet deck, but no major injuries."

"Or deaths?" Rex held Vaughan's gaze.

"Not on this yacht. Not on my watch." Vaughan cocked his head to one side. "Why do you ask?"

Rex shrugged. "Just curious what it takes to run an operation of this size and the pitfalls. You know, in case I decide to invest in one."

Vaughan turned to Rex's father, who stood to the side, his body stiff and his face unreadable to most.

Rex recognized the look. It was the same stony expression he used when he was angry and had to keep it together until he was somewhere he could let it out.

Vaughan held out his hand. "James, I'm glad you made it. It's been a while since you've attended one of my soirées."

James shook Vaughan's hand. "Thanks for the invitation."

Vaughan released James's hand and faced Rex. "It's been a pleasure, Rex. I hope to see you again soon." His gaze swung to the right. "Ah, there's my Chloe. I've neglected her for too long." He left them standing by the window and crossed the room to the woman in the silver dress.

Rex wanted to go after Vaughan and Holte and ask more questions, but he was on Vaughan's boat, surrounded by his hired security. Holte hadn't admitted that he'd lost a container, nor had he confessed to knowing what had been inside it.

Vaughan had the ability to pull a container off the ocean floor, then send out a small boat to protect it until they could retrieve it and send divers to take out Kimo, thus eliminating the last witness to the gruesome truth.

Without concrete evidence, Rex couldn't out-and-out accuse Vaughan and Holte of murder and attempted murder or of holding Alana hostage.

They still needed that camera for leverage. Not that Rex expected them to release Alana in trade for the camera and what was on it.

Most likely, they'd make sure Alana and Kimo would end up like the people they'd found in the container.

They needed to watch Vaughan and his people, get that camera and be there when they set up the exchange.

Vaughan slipped an arm around his partner, leaned close to her ear and said something that made her glance toward Rex and his father.

She gave a slight nod and walked with him out onto the deck.

"I think that's my cue to leave," Rex said quietly.

As he walked toward the door that led out onto the deck, his father followed.

"I shouldn't have brought you here," James Johnson said. "I don't know what you've gotten into, which is what I told Vaughan, but remember what I said. These people are untouchable."

"I take it that they have high-level politicians and authorities in their pockets, and they think they can get away with murder."

"I didn't say that," his father murmured. "You did."

"Understood." Rex stepped out onto the deck, his gaze sweeping the crowd, memorizing faces. Holte's was missing. Vaughan stood with several men, laughing at something someone had said.

A woman was being held hostage. People had died in that container, and the billionaires acted as if it was just another day.

"You can go around with your eyes closed to this kind of evil," Rex said. "I can't."

As Rex crossed the gangway, he reached into his pocket for the GPS tracker. He pretended to trip to distract anyone who might be looking as he tossed the tracker into La Petite Lolita, Vaughan's tender boat.

He regained his balance, straightened his suit and walked down the dock toward his truck.

A man in a dark jacket and black ball cap stepped off the deck of a catamaran and fell in behind him.

When Rex passed a sailboat, another man in a black jacket and ball cap fell in step with the catamaran guy.

Rex kept walking. When he arrived at his truck, the two men split and disappeared among the parked vehicles.

With a grin, Rex climbed into his truck and left the harbor. He hadn't gone far when another vehicle pulled in behind him. He pulled his cell phone out and called Devlin.

"That you behind me, Dev?"

"Roger," Devlin answered. "It was such a lovely evening, Teller and I decided to hang out at the harbor."

"Right," Rex said. "I fully expected a tail. Didn't think it would be you."

"Don't get too cocky, we have a tail behind us, and it's gaining speed," Devlin said. "We'll keep him busy.

But you might want to take Kimo somewhere besides your apartment, in case they've already looked up your address."

Rex's hand tightened on his cell phone. "Right. Thanks." He pressed the accelerator hard, gaining speed. Sixty, seventy, eighty and more. At the same time, he called Angel. "I've got a tail, and now that Holte and Lucien Vaughan know my name, they might pay a visit to my apartment. Move Kimo from my apartment to the safe house."

"The cottage you've been renovating?" Angel asked.

"Yes. It's not in my name. They'd have a hard time finding it in any records, especially overnight."

"On it," Angel said and ended the call.

The headlights falling further behind him swerved right and left, keeping the vehicle on their tail from passing.

When he normally turned onto Kuihelani Highway to enter Kahului on the side of town where his apartment was located, he took a left and followed Honoapilani Highway, leading into the northwest corner of town. Once he reached the beach road, he headed north.

He turned off onto a dirt road that led down to the beach and a cottage he'd been restoring a little at a time. It was close to being done on the inside, but other than replacing the roof, he'd purposely left the outside for last. Vegetation blocked it from view of the water, and the beach was surrounded by rocks, making it impossible for boaters to pull ashore.

Angel's SUV was parked beside the cottage.

Rex pulled up beside his vehicle, got out and started toward the cottage.

Angel stepped out onto the porch and called over his shoulder. "It's Rex."

Kimo shot through the door, down the steps and into Rex's arms.

He crushed her to him, burying his face in her dark hair.

"I was fine until they said you were being followed," she said, her voice muffled by his suit jacket.

"No, she wasn't," Leilani called out. "She paced the entire time you were gone."

Rex tipped up her chin and stared down into her dark eyes. They reflected the starlight, making them even more beautiful and mysterious. "I came back as soon as I could."

"It wasn't soon enough," she whispered.

He bent and pressed a brief kiss to her lips and then looked up at Angel and Leilani.

"Devlin called and let us know they didn't let the tail pass until well after they turned onto Kuihelani Highway."

"Good." Rex slipped an arm around Kimo's waist and walked with her up the stairs. "Are they on their way?"

"They are, after they make sure they're not being followed." Angel held open the door.

"Did you learn anything about where they're keeping Alana?" Kimo asked.

"As soon as Dev and Teller get here, I'll tell you what I know." He pushed into the cottage. "Right now, I could use the whiskey I didn't drink on board Lucien Vaughan's yacht."

CHAPTER 12

Kimo's heart still ached long after Rex debriefed his team. They'd included Hawk, Swede and Hank Patterson in the conversation.

Swede would gather more information, tapping into the dark web to learn about Lucien Vaughan and his dealings with billionaires and Saudi Princes. He'd also tap into any government agencies that might also be keeping tabs on the international playboy.

They agreed she and Rex would be all right to stay in the cottage that night, and they would all meet at Leilani's boat the following morning.

Angel and Leilani planned to camp out on the boat to make sure no one tried to sabotage it overnight.

After making a run into Kahului for pizza and some breakfast groceries, Devlin volunteered to sleep in his SUV at the entrance to the dirt road leading down to the cottage.

Angel and Leilani dropped Teller at his apartment on their way back to the Lahaina marina. Teller and Devlin would join the team the following morning to provide cover for the divers searching for the camera.

Alone with Rex, Kimo cleaned up after their late-night binge on pizza and stored the leftovers in the new seafoam-green refrigerator that looked like one out of the nineteen fifties but ran like a champ with a freezer sporting an ice machine.

The cottage had a nautical theme, with smooth, weathered wood flooring, a kitchen table made from a surfboard and benches on either side, made from surfboards, too. Netting and shells decorated the walls alongside prints and paintings of Hawaiian seashores and sunsets.

Everything was clean, neat and welcoming.

Kimo dragged her finger along the highly polished surface of the surfboard dining table. "Leilani says you did the renovations on this cottage."

Rex nodded, following behind her. "It's a work in progress."

"I like it. And I like the bedroom, where you've created bunks that look like fish netting but have real mattresses. It's a vacation home, ready for the next family to enjoy.

He smiled. "I like the master bedroom better."

"The sea captain's bed is impressive. Weren't beds on old sailing ships much smaller?" She turned to find him standing directly behind her—so close she could feel the heat from his body.

Or was that hers burning for him?

He caught up with her in the living room when she checked the lock on the door for the second time. She'd just reached for the lock when his hand closed over hers.

"It's locked," he said, his lips so close to her ear that his breath stirred tendrils of her hair.

Kimo closed her eyes and inhaled the cologne he'd worn for the evening.

She moved to the window where she could see outside as well as a reflection of herself and him when he came to step in behind her.

Rex had shed his jacket and tie but still wore the slacks and white shirt, unbuttoned now, but crisp and sexy against his tanned skin.

Though he stood behind her, she could see the hairs on his chest displayed in the open V of his shirt.

Too many times over the evening since his return, she'd wanted to reach out and touch him there. To feel the coarseness of those hairs and to press her cheek against them.

The kiss before he'd left on his dangerous mission had left her craving more. Yet, he hadn't made a move.

His hands moved to her shoulders. Slowly, gently, he turned her to face him. "Are you avoiding me?"

She looked up into his eyes. "No. Of course not."

"You haven't stood still since the others left." His brow furrowed. "Are you afraid of me for some reason?"

Unable to help herself, she raised her hand to his chest. "I'm not afraid of you," she said, adding softly, "I'm afraid of myself."

He gathered her carefully into his arms. "Why would you be afraid of yourself?" Rex bent to press a kiss to her forehead. "You're beautiful, caring and brave."

"I'm afraid of how scared I was when you left earlier. Afraid I'm starting to care too much." She rested her forehead against his chest. "Afraid you won't care as much for me in return." The last bit she let fade out, hoping he wouldn't actually hear her confession. At the same time, she wished he would.

"Oh, Kimo." He rested his chin on the top of her head, his arms holding her close but loosely enough she could easily break free. "How can two people learn to care for each other in such a short amount of time? I've had a hard time believing it can happen. I keep thinking it's an anomaly that will clear when the danger is over."

Kimo sighed. "I feel the same." She looked up into his eyes. "But if this is only for now, why not ride the wave? Take the dive. Live in the moment."

He cupped the back of her head and leaned down until their lips almost touched. "I don't want to leave a broken heart or leave with one."

"Rex Johnson, I didn't know you could be so poetic," she whispered. "I promise not to be broken-hearted if you promise the same."

"I'm not sure I can make that promise," he said and took her mouth in a gentle kiss.

Her hands slid up his chest to lock around the back of his neck, deepening their connection. She opened to him, seeking his tongue with hers, caressing, tasting...loving how it felt.

She wasn't sure she could make that promise either.

In the kiss... In the moment... She wasn't sure of anything but the desire... No... the *need* to be in his arms, to get as close as she could to this man who'd saved her life.

His hands slid down her back, cupped her bottom and lifted.

Kimo wrapped her legs around his waist as he turned and pressed her against the wall.

"I want you so much," he whispered against her mouth. "If you don't want the same, speak now."

"There's a captain's bed in the other room," she suggested, nibbling at his bottom lip. "Or up against the wall could be more exciting and challenging."

He chuckled. "I'll take that as a yes." He crushed her mouth with his and then carried her into the bedroom. Without turning, he kicked the door shut behind them.

A light burned on the nightstand, giving the room a warm glow. The bed was neatly made with a blue chambray comforter and fluffy white pillows.

Rather than lay her across the bed, he set her on her feet, captured her cheeks between his palms and stared down into her face. "Your eyes are like dark pools I could fall into and never find my way out."

She covered his hand, anchoring it against her cheek. "Keep it up, soldier," she said. "Flattery will get you everywhere." Kimo slid her hand along the opening of his shirt until she reached the middle button and flicked it open. One by one, she worked the rest of the way down to where the shirt disappeared into his trousers.

There, she unbuckled his belt, flicked the button open on his trousers and slid the zipper down.

Rex's body and cock stiffened.

Kimo covered him with her palm, a powerful sensation washing over her. She'd made him that hard. He wanted her.

She wanted him.

Rex parted the opening of her coverup, slid it over her shoulders and tossed it onto a chair.

Desire surged, filling Kimo with a sense of urgency. The need to be with him. Naked. Skin pressed against skin. His hard shaft buried deep inside of her.

Rex reached behind her, searching for the clasp on her bikini bra.

"This one doesn't work that way," she said and unhooked the clasp in the front. When her breasts sprang free, she pushed his shirt over his shoulder and pressed her nipples into the springy hairs on his chest.

Heat ignited at her core. Her patience stretched to the breaking point, she started to shimmy out of her bottoms.

Rex brushed her hands away and took over, easing her bikini bottoms over her hips and downward. As they crossed over her sex, Rex dropped to his knees, his hands smoothing over her buttocks, fingers tracing the crevice between. He leaned in to brush a kiss across her folds.

The more her bottoms lowered, the harder it became to breathe.

Kimo threaded her fingers into his hair, keeping him close, massaging his scalp and urging him to speed it up.

A kiss against one inner thigh was followed by another on the opposite thigh.

She eased her legs a little wider, her core pulsing, making her body ache with need.

By the time her bikini bottoms hit the floor, Kimo wanted to scream out his name. She kicked the suit aside.

Rex rose, toed off his shoes and dropped his

slacks. Once freed of his waistband, his shirt floated to the floor.

Finally, they stood naked in front of each other.

Too stimulated to be embarrassed, Kimo hungrily swept her gaze across his body.

Rex raised a hand to touch her long, loose hair. Then he brushed his fingers along the curve of her cheek, over her chin and down the long line of her throat, pausing at the pulse beating wildly at the base.

Though she wanted to touch him, to hold him and feel him inside her, she stood still, reveling in the sensations stirred by his touch.

"You're beautiful," he whispered as his fingers moved lower to trace the curve of her breast.

The nipple puckered and hardened, eager for his lips to wrap around it and suck gently.

Yet only his fingers moved over her body, sliding lower across her ribs, angling toward her center.

Her channel creamed, ready to take his fingers, eager to welcome his cock.

When he reached the apex of her thighs, he cupped her sex and dipped a finger inside.

Kimo's head dropped back, her eyes closing, and she moaned. "I might spontaneously combust."

"I'm on fire myself," he said and dipped in again.

She covered his hand and guided more fingers into her channel, one of her own joining his.

So wet.

So ready.

His hands left her so fast she whimpered.

Then she was being lifted and laid across the comforter.

Her knees fell to the sides, leaving her open to him.

Rex climbed onto the bed and between her legs, his hands planting on either side of her shoulders.

"I want you inside me," Kimo said. "Now."

"Soon," he said. "But first..." His lips took hers, his tongue sweeping past her teeth to tangle with hers in a long, sensuous joining, a precursor to what was to come.

When his mouth left hers, Kimo forced air past her vocal cords. "Now?"

He chuckled. "Not yet." Working his way down, he trailed his lips across her chin and down her neck, taking the same path as his fingers moments before.

When he sucked her breast into his mouth, she arched her back, willing him to take more.

He did, sucking hard and then gently flicking the tip until she squirmed beneath him.

After he treated her other breast to more of the same, she was beyond thinking. All she could do was ride the sensory storm raging through her body.

He eased down her body until his mouth hovered over her sex, his breath warm against her skin. With his thumbs, he parted her folds.

Kimo sucked in a breath that immediately lodged in her throat as his tongue swept over her clit.

An explosion of nerves sent shockwaves throughout her body, making her jerk and buck beneath him. "Oh my," she gasped. "Oh, oh..."

He flicked and swirled, sending her to the very edge and then launching her into a sea of ecstasy.

She rode wave after wave of her release, holding onto the joy for as long as she could before she collapsed onto the mattress. Still, it wasn't enough. Her empty channel, slick with her juices, ached to be filled. By Rex.

He climbed up her body, his cock nudging her entrance. He leaned over her, his body tense, his shaft thick and hard between her legs. "If you want to stop here, we can."

"Sweet Heaven, you can't stop now," she wailed.

"Wait," Rex said.

"Wait?" Kimo laughed. "Are you kidding me?"

He leaned over her to fumble in the nightstand. "Oh, thank God." He held up a little square packet.

Kimo let go of a sigh of relief. "I'm glad one of us is thinking." She took the packet from him, tore it open and rolled the condom over his engorged member. "Now, we're in business."

He settled again between her legs, dipping gently into her channel, teasing her with his hesitance.

She was having none of that. Her fingers sank

into his ass. With one quick tug, she brought him home.

Rex sucked in a sharp breath as he pressed all the way inside until fully sheathed, his balls nestling against her.

Kimo pushed him outward to the very tip and reversed his direction, bringing him back in. His thickness, the hardness of him sliding in and out, filled her completely.

He took over and moved inside her in a steady rhythm, increasing speed with every plunge.

As his body stiffened, he moved faster until he was pumping in and out, skin slapping against skin.

Kimo dug her heels into the mattress, raising her hips to meet him, taking him deeper.

Rex thrust hard and sank deep inside her; his body dropped down on her, his arms curling around her, holding her close as he came. Cock throbbing. Breath ragged. He buried his face in her neck and pressed his lips to the sensitive skin below her ear. "Wow," he whispered and took her earlobe between his teeth.

"Just wow?" she said, struggling to breathe under his weight, but not really caring. She liked his muscles pressed against her curves, his cock still filling her. She'd gladly die crushed beneath him than have him move anytime soon.

Rex leaned up on his arms.

Kimo sucked in a breath, filling her lungs as Rex stared down into her face. "Words can't begin to express what that was like for me. Like, wow, they seem sorely inadequate." He grinned and took her mouth in a long, sensuous kiss.

Then he rolled off her and gathered her in his arms, bringing her naked body up against his. "Are you all right?"

She pressed her cheek against his chest, listening to the thundering beat of his heart. "Better than all right. Better than anything I've experienced before."

He touched his lips to the top of her head. "While we're making promises..."

"I thought that was what we weren't doing," she reminded him.

"Let me finish," he said.

"Yes, sir." Kimo pulled one of his chest hairs.

"Hey," he admonished, "that was still attached."

"I know." She gave him a saucy smile.

"As I was saying," he began again while gathering her close. "Promise me that won't be the last time we do that." He leaned back and met her gaze. "Can you do that?"

Her heart warmed. "I promise." She smoothed her hand over his naked chest. "Would now be a good time to make good on that promise?" Her fingers slipped lower, aiming low on his body.

He captured her hand and brought it to his lips. "As much as I want to make good on that promise, we have to dive first thing in the morning. Which means, we need sleep."

Kimo sobered. "I know you're right, but I want so much more of the same as tonight."

"I think we can accommodate that and do one better."

"Better?" She shook her head. "I'm not sure I could handle better than perfection."

Rex chuckled. "Now you're giving me a big head."

She freed her hand from his and quickly slid it down his torso to grasp his cock. "That was my plan."

He kissed her, amazed at how fast she'd brought him back to a full erection. "What I meant by *better* was that it doesn't have to be the same. It can be even better if you're okay with changing things up."

Excitement flared inside her, taking her from almost drowsy to fully aroused in two seconds flat. "Sounds tempting. What did you have in mind?"

"This," he said.

He flipped her onto her belly and pulled her ass into the air, bringing her up on her knees, her face still planted on the comforter.

Her heart pounding against her ribs, her bare ass hiked up for Rex to see, touch or do anything he might want to do, Kimo laughed. "You might give a girl a little warning."

He rose on his knees behind her and smoothed his hands over her butt cheeks, reaching for her hips.

"I just want you to know that making love doesn't have to be the same every time."

"Obviously," she said, her breathing growing more ragged at the possibilities her position inspired.

"Are you up for a little adventure?" he asked, his hands clutching her hips.

"Yes, please," she whispered, already creaming, ready for him to take her in this new position.

Rex touched his cock to her entrance and tugged on her hips, pulling her backward. He slid in slowly and then moved in and out, increasing the tension, the speed and desire until her breath caught and held, waiting for the ultimate release.

Kimo's fingers curled into the comforter as he rode her, taking her back to that peak she'd teetered on minutes before. Without giving her time to process, he pushed her over the edge.

At the same time, Rex thrust once more and then leaned over her, capturing one of her breasts in his palm. One hand slid down her belly to slip between her folds. He strummed her clit while he came, making her entire body quiver.

They collapsed onto the bed.

Rex spooned Kimo, her butt tucked up against his groin, his cock nudging her ass. He stroked her arm in a slow, mesmerizing rhythm.

She sighed and closed her eyes. "I have to admit, I could do with more adventures like that."

"Good. I've got more where that came from."

Kimo smiled, yawned, then dragged Rex's arm around her and tucked it beneath her breasts. "Counting on it," she whispered, her eyelids drooping, her breathing slowing. "Tomorrow."

If they found the camera, didn't get killed exchanging it for Alana and survived the storm bearing down on Hawaii.

CHAPTER 13

REX JERKED awake from a wild dream and opened his eyes to shadows and starlight streaming in through a window. For a moment, he couldn't remember where he was. All he knew was that this wasn't his apartment.

Then memories flooded in. The yacht. Holte. Vaughan. His father.

Kimo standing naked in front of him, her long dark hair cascading over her shoulders and down her back.

He reached over to pull her close but found the space beside him empty, the pillow cool.

Kimo was gone.

Rex sat up, flung the sheet aside and rolled out of the bed onto his bare feet. The bedroom door stood open; more inky blue light shone through from the living area beyond.

His heart racing, every bad scenario running through his mind, Rex hurried in search of the woman who'd awakened in him desire and longing he'd never expected to find in any one woman.

His gaze desperately swept the room, praying she hadn't been taken away in the night.

Then he found her.

Her naked body was silhouetted in the starlight as she sat with her knees curled up on a window seat, staring out at what was left of the night.

He moved up behind her and rested his hands on her shoulders. "Couldn't sleep?"

She shook her head, her long, wavy hair brushing against his belly. "I feel guilty."

"Guilty?" he asked. "Why?"

She leaned her head back against him and raised a hand to cover the one resting on her shoulder. "Being with you, experiencing all the joy of being young, alive and free… It doesn't feel right when Alana is being held hostage. She's alone scared and—God forbid—maybe abused or tortured. I don't deserve to be happy when it's my fault she's not."

"It's not your fault," he assured her. "But I can't tell you how to feel when I've been there. I've lost buddies in battle and have spent years second-guessing my moves, knowing that if I had been the one on point that day, my buddy would've been alive today. Or if I'd only seen the enemy hiding in the shadows, I could've taken him out before he made a kill shot, taking out my friend. I blamed myself. In the back of my mind, I still do."

She turned, wrapped her arms around his waist and leaned her warm cheek against his torso. "I shouldn't have gone out that day," she whispered. "I should've been the one they took. Not Alana. I would gladly exchange my life for hers."

Her words hit Rex square in the gut. He drew her to her feet and wrapped his arms around her. "I can't let that happen." He laid his cheek against her hair, inhaling the scent of plumeria shampoo in her hair. "This fight isn't over. Alana is alive, and we have the chance to keep her that way. You have to believe that."

"What if we don't find my camera?" Kimo asked.

"We will," Rex said. "It's out there. We'll find it."

"We need to be there at first light." Kimo tipped her head back. "The storm comes tonight. The seas will get rougher the closer it gets."

Rex cupped her cheeks and bent to brush his lips across hers. "Then we'll have to find the camera early and make the trade before the storm hits."

Kimo curled her hands around the back of Rex's neck. "I have a feeling this isn't going to end easily."

Rex had that same feeling. It sat like a heavy rock in his gut. Once they had the camera, he'd work with Hawk and their entire team to ensure Kimo's safety and bring Alana back alive. Then they'd work on exposing and bringing down the network of human traffickers.

He kissed Kimo and held her close, enjoying a few more seconds with her body pressed to his. "I could hold you like this twenty-four seven and still not get enough."

"Same," she said with a sigh. "Dawn won't be for another hour..."

Rex didn't need any more encouragement than that. He swept Kimo up in his arms and carried her into the bedroom, where he made sweet love to her, bringing her to her own release before slaking his own desire. They showered together, exploring more of each other's bodies and then dressed for the dive ahead.

Thankfully, Rex had a spare swimsuit in the cottage for the days he worked there and then went out to cool off in the ocean.

Once again, Kimo wore the red bikini Rex had grown to love. Shrugging into the beachy coverup, she slipped her feet into flipflops and hooked her arm through his. "Ready?" she said with a determined tilt of her chin.

"I am," he responded, planting a kiss on the tip of her nose. "Let's find that camera."

On the way out the door of the cottage, Rex spotted the little sports camera he'd bought for when he went snorkeling off the beach in front of the cottage. He snagged the little camera and tucked it into the pocket of his swim trunks, thinking it might be a good idea to record their dive this time. If other divers attacked them, recording them might help to identify them.

They stepped out of the cottage into darkness with stars still twinkling overhead and a slight wind stirring among the palms. They had just enough time to reach the Lahaina marina, load the gear and get out on the water by the time the sun rose above the horizon.

Rex handed Kimo up into the passenger seat and slid into the driver's seat. He texted Devlin they were on their way. When he drove out onto the highway, Devlin's SUV fell in behind him.

They made the drive in silence. Kimo braided her hair while Rex worked through scenarios in his thoughts, going over and over potential attacks, ways to search for the missing camera and how he would stay near Kimo no matter what.

The woman had started to mean more to him than just a client. It wasn't about the sex, though that had been beyond anything he could have imagined.

He liked being with her.

Kimo wasn't a silly woman, worried about makeup and fashion trends. Besides being an expert diver, she was a talented photographer who'd built a business on her own, with no help from family wealth or connections. Plus, she valued family and friendship above all.

His life in the Army had taught Rex the value of friends, and how good friends were family. For the first time in his life, he could imagine having a family of his own. With children. Maybe a little girl with light brown skin and dark eyes, running across the sand, her long, flowing dark hair streaming out behind her.

His breath seized in his lungs. Rex shot a glance toward Kimo, suddenly afraid of the task in front of them. Afraid of the thought of losing her when their relationship had barely gotten started.

She turned and gave him a tight smile. "I don't think I could do any of this without you. Thanks for being here."

He took her hand and held onto it. "I wouldn't want to be anywhere else."

Rex parked the truck in the parking lot near the marina and walked with Kimo to the Windsong Tours slip as the gray light of dawn crept over Lahaina.

Devlin followed.

Leilani, Angel and Teller were already aboard the tour boat, arranging tanks and BCDs.

"Run into any trouble last night?" Rex asked as he stepped onto the tour boat.

Teller shook his head. "None. It was a little unsettling."

Angel looked up from where he was checking the

gauge on a regulator after having hooked it to the tank. "I felt the same."

Rex turned to offer a hand to Kimo as she stepped onto the boat.

"It was a strange night." Kimo snorted softly. "Like the calm before the storm." Her lips twisted into a grimace. "Pun intended."

Leilani shook her head. "Needless to say, none of us got much sleep. I couldn't stop thinking about Alana."

"Me either." Kimo crossed to where Angel was going over the gear and did a second pass.

"If everyone's ready, let's go." Leilani nodded to where Devlin stood on the dock. "Let her loose."

Devlin removed the line from the cleat, tossed it onto the boat then stepped across.

Once they were all inside, Leilani fired up the engine and drove the boat slowly out of the slip, through the no-wake zone and into the harbor.

Once they left the harbor, they encountered choppy seas. The swells and waves were bigger than the day before. Dark clouds hung over the sky to the west, harbingers of the storm moving ever closer to the islands.

No one on board attempted conversation. Wind and motor noise made it hard enough to communicate. They all seemed to focus on the task ahead as the divers dressed in wetsuits.

Teller and Osgood checked their rifles and handguns.

Rex had his dive knife and managed to hook the underwater sports camera to his BCD vest. He hoped the batteries were charged and ready. As soon as they hit the water, he'd turn it on.

As they neared the shipping container's coordinates, Leilani slowed the tour boat, bringing it to a halt.

Rex helped Kimo into her BCD and buckled her straps.

Kimo returned the favor.

After she buckled his BCD in place and checked his gauges, he pulled her close and kissed her. "Be careful out there and stay with me."

She gave him a tight smile. "You be careful, too. I kind of like having you around."

Kimo turned to the divers. "I want to do this differently this time. I've been thinking about what happened and where we were when we were attacked. I'm going to try to recreate the directions we were heading to the best of my memory. Bear with me and follow."

Leilani and Angel were first into the water.

Kimo and Rex followed, switching the little camera on as he submerged.

Kimo kept close to the surface and started out swimming at an angle away from the reef for several yards. She slowed, brought her head out of the water, glanced around and turned back toward the reef, again at an angle, not directly toward it.

Now, she was swimming directly for the reef, kicking harder and faster.

When she came within several feet of the dark mass of rocks, she slowed and motioned for Leilani and Angel to search to the right.

Kimo turned left and followed the line of rocks, moving slowly at first.

Rex swam beside her, alternating between looking ahead and keeping an eye on their six.

Something shiny caught his attention.

It must have caught Kimo's eye at the same time because she shot ahead.

They arrived together near a massive rock outcropping. As they fought the current and waves pushing them into the jagged edges, they reached down and brushed away sand, revealing the tank and BCD Kimo had abandoned.

Rex's gut clenched when he saw the bullet hole in the tank. Had it been a foot higher, the bullet would have struck Kimo in the back of her head.

Having found the BCD, they left it standing in the sand and dug all around it, looking for the camera.

When no amount of digging unearthed it, Kimo moved over the rocks.

Rex followed, searching the cracks and crevices while trying to keep from being scraped across the jagged surfaces.

Suddenly, Kimo disappeared behind a large boulder.

His heart lurching into his throat, Rex hurried to follow.

He found her struggling to reach into a crevice, her fins flipping, as she tried to push deeper.

When she seemed to be making no progress, he tugged on her tank.

Kimo's head came up, and she hovered over the crevice, jabbing her finger downward.

Rex moved over the spot and stared down.

A camera lay wedged several feet down between rocks. Too far for Kimo to reach, but maybe not for him.

Rex leaned into the crevice, stretching his arm as far as he could reach, which was at least two inches short of snagging the strap on the camera.

The bulk of the tank and BCD kept him from getting deeper into the crevice.

When he came up, Kimo tried to dive in to try again.

Rex stopped her and held up a hand for her to wait. He pointed to himself and down at the crevice. He would try again. Then he unbuckled the straps on his BCD.

Kimo's hand closed over his, and she shook her head.

Rex grabbed her fingers and squeezed them gently. He set her hand away from him and completed the task of shrugging out of his BCD and tank, careful to keep the regulator in his mouth as he set it on a nearby rock. He took her hand and placed it on the tank. Motioning for her to hold onto it.

When he was sure she understood, he took a deep breath, removed the regulator from his mouth and dove into the crevice.

He pulled himself deeper and stretched his arm into where the gap narrowed. The tips of his fingers curled around the strap. He tugged gently, afraid that if he jerked it upward, it would wedge itself into the rock. The camera moved several inches and jammed.

Rex released the pressure on the strap, letting the camera fall an inch. With a twist of his hand, he turned the camera slightly and lifted again.

Again, the camera stopped where the edge of a rock jutted out.

His lungs starting to burn, Rex kicked his fins, moving to a little different angle over the camera. He let the camera drift downward and then brought it straight up, not at an angle, avoiding the jutting rock.

By the time he had the camera free of the tight space, his lungs burned with the need to breathe.

A hand clamped on his ankle, dragging him upward.

When his head cleared the crevice, Kimo was there, placing her regulator into his mouth.

Rex sucked in a breath and let it out, then sucked in another as he held up the camera.

Kimo hugged him hard and briefly.

They buddy-breathed over to the other BCD and tank. Kimo took the camera, attached it to her BCD and helped Rex into his tank.

When he was breathing normally with his own regulator, he sent the message, *Found it,* and followed with *Surface Now.*

With one hand on the camera, holding it snuggly to her chest, Kimo reached for Rex's hand. She squeezed it and then swam back to the damaged BCD that would serve as additional evidence of treachery.

Rex hooked a hand through the harness.

As they slowly ascended, Rex kept an eye out for motorboats overhead and attack divers below.

Leilani and Angel joined them as the tour boat circled and stopped close to them.

The waves had grown rougher in the time they'd been down. Devlin had to help them out of the water and onto the deck.

When all were safely aboard, Teller turned the boat around and headed for the Lahaina marina.

They stripped out of their gear and stowed it safely. Rex removed his underwater sports camera from the BCD vest, glad they hadn't run into any attackers during their dive. He shoved it into his pocket and sat beside Kimo.

Leilani took over at the helm.

Kimo sat with the camera in her lap, pushing

buttons, her brow furrowing. She glanced up and shook her head. "I can't get it to work."

Rex held out his hand. "Let me see."

She handed it to him, pushed to her feet and started stripping out of her wetsuit.

"They said they wanted the camera. They didn't say anything about a requirement for it to work." Devlin pointed out from his position near the back of the tour boat, where he held onto a post for balance and his rifle should anyone slip up behind them.

Rex tried to turn on the camera. "Most likely the battery is dead."

"My charger and spare battery were on the dive boat they took." Kimo shook her head and turned away.

Curious about how the camera worked, Rex turned knobs, flicked switches and opened the compartment that held the storage devices. This camera used a similar SD card as his smaller sports camera.

Rex pulled his little camera out of his pocket and opened the disk storage compartment. The SD cards were the same size, if not the same storage capacity.

Kimo had moved to stand near Leilani, staring at the path ahead, talking with her about Alana and the last time they'd had a girls' night out.

Rex switched the SD cards in the cameras and closed the compartments. As Devlin had pointed out, the trade was for the camera. Rex stuffed his camera into his pocket.

Leilani drove the tour boat into the Lahaina harbor and slowed as she neared the slip. "We've got company."

Rex stood. He'd noticed the Maui Police Department vehicle parked in front of the Windsong slip.

"Please, don't let it be Detective Sykes," Kimo murmured as she rose to stand beside Rex.

At that moment, Detective Sykes stepped out of the vehicle.

"Isn't he the jerk who raked Kimo over the coals?" Leilani asked.

Rex nodded. "That's the one."

"Should I park or make a run for it?" Leilani whispered, without moving her lips.

"He's seen us," Angel said. "You might as well park."

"It's not like we're guilty of anything," Devlin said, having stowed the weapons in their gear bags and beneath one of the benches.

Leilani pulled into the slip. Angel jumped out and hooked the line over the cleat on the dock, securing the boat.

Rex stepped off the boat onto the dock. "Detective Sykes, what brings you out so early?"

"I could ask you the same." The man's gaze looked past Rex to land on Kimo. "Ah, I see you found your camera, Ms. Kealoha." He held out his hand. "I'll take that."

Kimo's face blanched as she clutched the camera to her chest. "It's mine."

The detective wiggled his fingers impatiently. "You're the one who reported a mysterious shipping container. Did you or did you not take photos of the supposed container?"

"It was there." Kimo's brow lowered.

"You didn't answer my question." Detective Sykes skewered her with his glance. "If there are photos on that camera, I have to enter them as evidence."

"But I need the camera," she said. "I have to have it."

"You can get it back after we've had a chance to review any evidence of your claim."

"But that could be weeks," Kimo cried.

The detective shrugged. "Or months. Hand it over."

Kimo didn't move.

The desperation in her eyes made Rex want to pull her close and save her from the pain, but he couldn't. Not now. He stepped back onto the deck and held out his hand. "Give me the camera, Kimo," he said softly.

Tears welled in her eyes. "You know what it means," she whispered. "I can't."

Rex's hand covered hers, holding her camera to

her chest. "You have to." Then, so quietly only she would hear, he said, "Trust me."

For a long moment, she held tightly to the camera. Finally, she loosened her hold and let him take it from her.

Rex handed the camera to the detective. "Is that all you wanted from Ms. Kealoha, or are you going to bully her again?"

Detective Sykes took the camera and stared down his nose at the men and women on the boat. "I'm only doing my job. You'd do best to keep comments like that to yourself."

"Or what?" Rex challenged.

The detective's eyes narrowed to slits. "Don't test me, Johnson. Your father's money can't buy your way out of everything." With that parting jab, the detective climbed back into his vehicle and drove away.

Rex turned back to Kimo, his heart squeezing hard in his chest.

The look of betrayal radiating from her expression was almost as harsh as her whispered words, "What about Alana?"

Rex glanced over his shoulder to make certain Detective Sykes had truly left. When the man's vehicle had moved out of sight, Rex hooked Kimo's arm and led her inside the tour boat.

The others followed. No one said a word.

Rex pulled his camera from his pocket, opened

the compartment and dropped the SD disk into Kimo's hand. "Sykes might have the right camera, but he has the wrong disk."

CHAPTER 14

KIMO CURLED her fingers around the disks and looked up into Rex's eyes. The tears she'd been holding back, thinking the camera and her trade for Alana were gone, fell silently down her cheeks.

Rex gathered her into his arms.

She pressed her cheek to his chest and let the rest of the tears go. When they'd played out, she wiped her cheeks and looked up again. "How did you know to switch them?"

"Instinct? Luck?" He wiped her cheek with his thumb. "Either way, we have the right disk. Even better, the detective won't know he has the wrong one for a while because I had my little camera recording during our dive today."

Angel clapped a hand on Rex's back. "Well played."

Dev and Teller both grinned and nodded.

"So, we have the right disks," Leilani said. "The kidnappers specifically wanted the camera and the information on it. How do they want you to deliver them?"

Kimo shook her head. "I don't know."

Rex's cell phone chirped. He hurried to grab it from where he'd left it on the bench. "It's Swede," he said as he answered. "Hey, Swede, let me put you on speaker." He hit the button.

Swede's voice sounded, "Did you find it?"

Rex looked to Kimo.

"Yes," Kimo said.

"Good deal," Swede said. "Hawk's on the line with us. I'll make this as quick as I can. I know you want to get moving on the trade to get your friend back, but you need to know what you're up against."

Kimo's fist tightened around the disk in her hand as she looked around the group assembled. "We're listening."

"I bounced around on the dark web looking for anything I could find on Marcus Holte and Lucien Vaughan. I found info on both men. Holte appeared in a number of photos of him with business partners and associates in the shipping trade, as well as attending parties hosted by guess who?"

"Lucien Vaughan," Rex said.

"Right." Swede continued. "The more I looked into Vaughan, the more photos I found with him and a number of very wealthy and influential people, which I'd mentioned before. I also found that he has a network of people in each of his prime locations that run interference for him to keep him out of trouble with law enforcement and other federal agencies."

"Like the Coast Guard?" Rex asked.

"Exactly," Swede responded. "As well as local police departments, state officials and more. Some of the sources say he drives it from top down."

Kimo blew out a sharp breath. "Meaning he has people in high positions clearing the way for him to commit crime with impunity."

"Did any of the sources on the dark web mention human trafficking?" Rex asked.

"Yes. Vaughan is known for staffing his yacht and his home in the States and Paris with young women from all over the world. His records show they're all over eighteen."

Rex frowned. "They're not. I spoke with a Romanian girl on his yacht. She told me she was only fourteen years old."

Kimo shook her head. "Children."

"That's right," Swede said. "The friends he invites to his parties don't just turn a blind eye. They participate in his activities and the cover-up. Vaughan's yacht and some of his various residences had been involved in several FBI sting operations and the authorities had come up with nothing. They'd suspected he'd gotten adequate warning before the inspections took place. Enough to hide his crimes diver propulsion vehicles."

"They had a mole inside," Kimo said.

"My father called it," Rex said. "Vaughan and his cronies are untouchable. They can get away with murder."

"And they have, several times, according to the dark web. Whenever someone thinks they have evidence that can stick, they disappear, or their bodies are found before they can testify in court."

"Jesus," Kimo whispered. "Which could mean that the bodies in that shipping container could've been young girls, lost because someone warned them about a surprise inspection." Acid roiled in her belly.

"Which means we need to catch Vaughan in the act," Rex said.

Hawk's voice came on. "He wouldn't get his hands dirty. He'd send in his henchmen."

"How do we smoke him out?" Angel asked.

"Call his bluff," Kimo said.

Rex frowned down at her. "What do you mean?"

"Whoever is holding Alana must have a link or contact with Vaughan," Kimo reasoned. "Vaughan doesn't want the evidence to get out, no matter how many people he has under his thumb. We go directly to Vaughan and call his bluff." She met Rex's gaze. "Make him collect the evidence himself."

"If I don't see him with Alana alive, when I go to

make the trade," she said, "I leave and turn the evidence over to someone who isn't on his payroll."

"You don't get it," Angel said. "He's not going to let you or Alana get out of this alive. You're witnesses. If you go alone to trade the disk for Alana's life, Vaughan gets the disk and kills both of you."

Her heart sank. "Then how do I get Alana back without either one of us being killed?"

"I don't know," Rex said. "All I know is that you can't turn the disk over to Vaughan. If he has that, he has no reason to keep you and Alana alive."

Kimo held out her hand. "Then maybe you should hold onto this." She dropped the disk into Rex's hand. "Though we still have no way of getting Alana out of Vaughan's clutches."

"I'm thinking about it," Rex said. "Even if we manage to free Alana, the two of you are witnesses who've seen the bodies in the submerged storage box. Vaughan won't want loose ends. He won't trust the two of you to keep quiet about what you saw. You'll never be safe."

"They won't keep Alana alive forever," Kimo said.

Rex nodded. "Whatever we decide, we have to do it quickly. By now, he'll have figured out you found the camera. Even if he thinks he has the evidence, he won't want you running around telling everyone he's a murderer."

"Then maybe I should go ahead and offer to make

the trade, but demand I do it with Vaughan, not his thugs."

Rex shook his head. "You'll have the same end result."

"Then what can I do?"

"Rooster, Bennett, Logan and Ingram are inbound from Oahu," Hawk said. "They should be arriving at the airport around now. I'll land within the next ten minutes. I suggest we—"

A loud boom shook the boat.

Rex shoved Kimo down onto the deck and covered her body with his.

Screams sounded as the smoke cleared.

The Brotherhood Protectors leaped to their feet. Rex helped Kimo up while Angel gave Leilani a hand.

"What the hell was that?" Leilani cried.

Flame rose from a shop halfway down the pier.

A woman raced out of a burning building, her clothes tattered, her face smudged. "Help! Please help me," she cried. "My husband is trapped inside."

Angel, Devlin and Teller leaped onto the dock and ran toward the woman as she turned and ran back into the burning building.

Rex leaped out onto the dock, took two steps and stopped, his gaze following his teammates. Then he glanced back at the two women on the tour boat. He hesitated.

Kimo waved at him. "Go! You have to help."

Rex's attention shifted back to his teammates as

they reached the building and dove inside. Flames rose from the roof, smoke billowing into the sky.

The front of the building collapsed.

Kimo and Leilani gasped.

A weird feeling washed over Rex as he ran toward the burning building. How many explosions happened around this marina. As he stepped into the building to save his friends he almost turned around to go back out. Was this all a set up?

"Oh, my God. Angel!" Leilani cried and leaped out onto the dock. "We have to help him." She ran after Rex.

Kimo hurried to follow but stumbled over her flip-flops. A gentleman in a Hawaiian shirt, ball cap and sunglasses, rushed over to help steady her by gripping her elbow.

"Thank you," she said. "I'm okay now, you can let go."

"Sorry, lady. I can't do that." He released her arm, clamped a hand over her mouth and jabbed a needle in her neck.

Kimo jerked away, staggered and would have fallen, except the man who'd helped her scooped her up in his arms and carried her away from the fire, Rex and the others.

As he stepped down into a small boat and laid her on the back seat, she knew she should fight, but none of her muscles responded. When she opened her mouth to scream, her vision faded to black.

. . .

Rex leaped over the fallen awning and ran into the burning building. Smoke assaulted his lungs and burned his eyes.

Devlin led the woman who'd screamed past Rex, ducking low to avoid the smoke.

Angel appeared, holding a man up on one side with Teller on the other.

"Anyone else inside?" Rex asked.

"No," Angel said. "We need to get out. The roof's about to give."

Leilani rushed in behind Rex. "Angel!"

"Get Leilani out of here," Angel said, his voice raspy.

Rex gripped Leilani's arm. "Come on. We need to clear a path." He helped her over the fallen awning and out into the open air.

Angel and Teller followed with the injured man. No sooner had they stepped away from the building than the roof collapsed inward, sending up a firestorm of flames and ash, whipped higher in the air by a blustery wind.

Angel and Teller helped the man away from the fire and eased him to the ground.

Leilani flung herself into Angel's arms. "You could've been in there when the roof gave."

"I wasn't."

Rex glanced around. "Where's Kimo?"

Leilani's head spun toward the tour boat. "She was right behind me."

Rex ran back to the tour boat and jumped on board, his gut telling him what he already knew.

She wasn't there.

His team and Leilani spent the next five minutes searching the marina, the boats and the vehicles parked nearby.

Kimo was gone.

Shoving his hand through his hair, Rex fought the urge to roar his frustration. He'd taken his focus off her for a minute. Maybe two. Now, she was gone.

He reached into his pocket for his cell phone and found the SD disk instead.

If Vaughan had her, he'd kill her—unless he thought he could use her as he'd used Alana.

As leverage.

The others gathered around Rex.

"You think Vaughan took her?" Angel asked. He already had his phone out. "I'll let Hawk know."

Rex dug his cell phone out of his other pocket and called Swede. As soon as the tech guru answered, Rex said. "I need Lucien Vaughan's personal phone number."

"What happened?"

"He had someone set off an explosion in a building here at the marina."

"Sounds like a diversion," Swede surmised.

"While we were helping people out of the burning building, they snatched Kimo."

"You think calling Vaughan will get her back?" Swede asked.

In the background, Rex heard the rapid tap of fingers on a keyboard. "I have to try. He might have Kimo and Alana, but I have the SD card with the pictures of the bodies inside. I need to make a copy, but I don't have a laptop or alternate means to duplicate the card at this time."

"He'll want the card." Swede tapped a key louder than the others. "Just sent you his number and brought Hank in on the call."

"Hank, I need you to call in all your favors and get the FBI, CIA, Interpol, national guard and state and local police ready. I'm going after Kimo and Alana and taking Vaughan down."

"He'll be a valuable asset, naming all the people involved in his operation and all the men who've taken advantage, aka raped, underage girls he's been trafficking," Hank said.

"You're telling me to bring him in alive?"

"Just saying, there are others involved who are as guilty as sin," Hank said.

"I'll keep that in mind, but I'm not risking Kimo or Alana's lives to save that bastard."

"Understood," Hank said. "Hawk's on his way. I can send more men from my team here in Montana."

"Not enough time. Vaughan will run. I can't let

him do that. We'll have to hit hard and fast to stop him before he leaves the islands."

"I'll make the calls," Hank promised.

"Just make sure it's not to the people loyal to Vaughan."

"Got it," Hank said. "Out here."

"Good luck. If you need anything," Swede said, "I'll be available twenty-four-seven."

"Thanks. Out here." Rex ended the call and brought up the text message with Vaughan's personal cell phone number.

Leilani touched Rex's arm. "Are you just going to call Vaughan and demand he give Kimo back?"

"No, I'm going to make a deal with the devil." Rex touched the number, initiating the call.

He fully expected the call to go to voicemail; however, a familiar voice sounded in his ear. "Who the hell is this, and how did you get this number?"

"Lucien Vaughan, Rex Johnson here. You have something I want. I have something you want. You're a man used to making deals. I have one for you."

"I'm sorry, I don't make deals over the phone. If you'd like to meet in person, I'll listen."

Rex's hand tightened on the phone, anger simmering just beneath the surface. He wished he could reach through the phone and strangle the man for all the girls he'd trafficked, abused or killed. Rex couldn't let Vaughan hurt or kill Kimo. If he wasn't already in love with the beautiful photographer, he was well on his way.

It was as if he'd waited all his life for someone like Kimo. He'd be damned if he let a douche bag like Lucien Vaughan make her disappear.

"Oh, you'll listen," Rex said. "You may think you have the lid on the case of the missing shipping container and its contents. You have Alana, now Kimo and Kimo's camera." He paused for effect. "What you don't have is the SD card with the images of the shipping container and the bodies of the people you sentenced to death when you dropped it into the ocean."

"I don't know what you're talking about. Who would dump a container full of girls into the ocean?"

"A monster," Rex said. "You." He noted that he hadn't told Vaughan that the bodies inside had been girls. Yet the man appeared to know. Because he'd ordered them put there and dropped into ocean."

"That's a serious allegation," he said. "One you can't prove because it isn't true."

"When I release the SD to the FBI, CIA, Interpol and every news station in the world, it will have your name on it. The owner of that container will go to court. To save his own skin, they'll cut him a deal to name the man behind the abuse and trafficking of young girls. Your billionaire friends will turn their backs on you and pretend they never knew you or what you were up to. Your days of princes giving you yachts will be over. Are you willing to trade your gold and freedom for iron and an orange jumpsuit?"

"I can't have you spreading lies about me. It's slander. I won't stand for it. You'll be the one to go to jail. Not me."

"Your network of snitches and stooges inside law enforcement and government entities won't be able to save you," Rex promised.

"You have something to show me, bring it to me. I'll be the judge of it."

"I'll bring the disk, but if anything happens to Alana or Kimo, the deal's off."

"Again, I have nothing to hide. I don't know anything about these Alana and Kimo persons, but I take pride in protecting my reputation and that of the people with whom I associate. If you come after me, I'll make sure you go to jail for a very long time. This conversation is over."

"Vaughan, don't you hang up—"

The call ended.

Rex cocked his arm, ready to throw his phone into the ocean.

A hand caught his wrist. Angel stepped in front of him, holding up his own phone. On it was a screen with a crooked line and a dot at one end, making the line even longer.

"Your tracking device is on the move. Did you put it on Kimo?" Angel asked.

Rex frowned at the image. "No. I dropped it into

Vaughan's boat, the La Petite Lolita. His version of a dinghy." He stared at the image.

"It left Lahaina Harbor about the time Kimo disappeared," Angel said.

Rex frowned down at the dot moving further and further away. "Is it headed toward Maalaea Bay?"

Angel shook his head. "No."

"I just got off the phone with the harbor master," Leilani said. "The Dancing Lolita left Maalaea Bay this morning."

"Destination?" Rex barked.

"Hong Kong," Leilani responded.

Rex glanced around. "I need a boat. A fast one."

"Give me a minute," Leilani said. "I have a friend I can call."

A dark SUV raced toward them.

Angel grabbed Leilani and shoved her out of the way. The others scattered as the vehicle came to a screeching halt a few short feet away.

Hawk jumped out of the driver's seat. "I just heard the news. We're here to help."

The other doors on the SUV opened. Rooster, Bennett, Logan and Ingram, the Brotherhood Protectors team members from Oahu, got out.

"I think they're taking Kimo to Vaughan's yacht," Rex said. "Supposedly, it's heading for Hong Kong. We have to stop it before it leaves the islands."

Hawk nodded. "And before the storm hits."

"The yacht will have to be stationary for them to transfer Kimo from the dinghy and to bring the dinghy on board. Loading a boat the size of La Petite Lolita in choppy water won't be easy. It'll take time."

"Wouldn't they just abandon it?" Devlin asked.

"Not if Vaughan is clinging to the pretense that he knows nothing about Kimo and Alana's disappearances. And he'll need the smaller boat to get to and from ports too shallow to receive the Dancing Lolita."

"I have a boat," Leilani cried out. "A retired Coastie is loaning it to us."

Hope bloomed in Rex's gut. "Is it fast?"

"JD bought an old RHIB—Rigid Hull Inflatable Boat—at a military surplus auction and refurbished it," Leilani said.

"It'll be faster than Vaughan's little boat in rough seas." Hawk, the former Navy SEAL, would know, having trained in similar watercraft.

"We need to get there before they fully load Vaughan's boat onto the yacht," Rex said. "It would be best if they didn't see us coming. The element of surprise would help us infiltrate the boat before they know it's happening."

Hawk grinned. "I have the goods." He waved a hand toward the rear of the SUV.

Rex followed.

Inside the back, several containers were stacked

to the ceiling. Hawk grabbed one and pulled it out onto the ground. "I wasn't exactly sure what we'd need, so I brought some of everything from our arsenal on the Big Island. Since you were doing a lot of diving, I brought the latest addition of tools we could use for underwater operations and exploration."

He popped the top of the container. Inside were a couple of diver propulsion vehicles, much like those used by Vaughan's divers.

If they could get close enough in the boat, they could use the propulsion vehicles to take them the rest of the way without being spotted until they breached the yacht and subdued Vaughan's security team.

"Look." Leilani pointed toward a boat approaching the dock. "There's JD now."

"We'll need tanks and BCDs," Angel said.

"In the shop," Leilani said. "We have enough to outfit all of you."

They divided up, some going with Angel and Leilani to collect the diving gear the team would need, while the others helped unload the SUV.

Hawk had brought five DPVs, waterproof radio headsets, four stun guns, zip ties and duct tape. From another box, Rex pulled out a black bag. "What's this?"

"It's a tactical boarding ladder, complete with a launching unit and grappling hook."

Rex grunted. "Perfect. We might need that."

"Let's get this stuff onto JD's boat," Angel said. "We're running out of time. All this stuff will be useless if we don't get to Vaughan's yacht before he punches out."

Between all of them, they had the boat loaded and ready to go in minutes.

When JD offered to pilot the boat, Hawk decided to let him. He would stay back far enough from the yacht that they wouldn't see him or target his boat. That left the entire team available to board the yacht, rescue the women and capture Vaughan.

Twenty minutes after Kimo disappeared, the team left Lahaina harbor, suited up in wetsuits and scuba gear. They headed out into choppy water. JD and the RHIB handled the waves like a champ. Rex and his team held on tight, the heavy gear making it more challenging. They couldn't afford to lose someone and take the time to go back and get them.

The boat with the tracking device was headed for the deserted island of Kahoolawe, a former military bombing range, not an island reserve revered by the native Hawaiians. What normally would have taken the little boat twenty to thirty minutes to get to Kanapou Bay, where it appeared to be heading, was taking it forty minutes or more.

Rex hoped that with his many hours of experience driving his own boat, the old Coastie would get them there in half that time. He hoped Vaughan didn't get trigger-happy and dispose of the witnesses before the Brotherhood Protectors could get there and keep it from happening.

By the time they came within range of the bay, the waves were heavier, making it harder to hold onto the RHIB. The team doubled up on the DPVs, Rex being the only one with his own. He also took the tactical boarding ladder kit. Taking point, he would climb aboard near the rear, take out any security guards watching over the low, rear deck and drop a ladder in for the others to climb aboard.

As soon as he was ready, he dropped into the water, fired up the DPV and followed the coast of the little island close to the surface until he could see into the bay where the Dancing Lolita lay anchored. For a moment, he studied the yacht.

The crane moved slowly, reaching out over the side of the yacht where the La Petite Lolita waited to be hoisted aboard.

If they hurried, they could board the yacht before they finished loading the spare boat.

Rex glanced back at his team, which wasn't too far behind him. With two men per DPV, they met more resistance and thus moved more slowly.

That worked for him. It would take time for him to scale the side of the ship on the rope ladder, neutralize resistance and prepare the deck for the team's ascension.

Technically, it was daytime, but the thick, dark clouds blocked the sun, making the day dusky.

Rex powered toward the opposite side of the boat from where all the action was taking place with the loading of the smaller boat.

Once there, he pulled out the grappling hook with the thin rope ladder attached, studied the rim of the lowest level, aimed and fired. The grappling hook landed on the deck on the other side of the rail. Rex took up the slack until the hook seated firmly against the rail. He patted the pocket with the little sports camera keeping the SD card dry. I he had to save Kimo's life, he'd trade the card and his soul to keep her safe. He'd made a copy on his spare laptop while at the cottage. If he had to trade the disk in his pocket, all wasn't lost.

He tied his heavy scuba gear to the bottom of the ladder and started up, carefully placing his feet on the metal rungs as the boat rocked. Each movement made him swing back and forth. Slowly, he moved up the side of the boat until he could peer over the rail.

No one moved on this side. He glanced up but couldn't see anyone looking down from levels above. Rex pulled himself up and over the rail, dropping low on the deck. Staying close to the walls and ducking below windows, he made his way to the back of the vessel, where he'd spied at least one man standing guard, holding a rifle.

As Rex approached the man, he saw him stiffen and lean toward the edge to stare down into the water.

Pulling the stun gun from his utility belt, he crept up to the guard.

When he was three feet from his target, the man turned.

"Sorry, bro," Rex said and tapped him with the stun gun. The guy dropped with little more than a squeak. Knowing the effects wouldn't last long, Rex dragged the guy under the overhang, pulled duct tape from the pocket of his wetsuit, tore off a piece and stretched it across the man's mouth. He flipped the guy onto his belly and secured his wrists with a zip tie, then applied another to his ankles.

He moved quickly and efficiently, securing the man in less than a minute. Then he hurried back to the edge of the dive platform and dropped the metal ladder into the water.

One by one, his team climbed aboard.

Rex helped them out of the gear, stowing it safely beneath the overhang, out of view of any casual observers or security personnel.

When they were ready, they moved out.

Hawk would take the bulk of the team up one deck at a time.

Angel and Rex would go up to the deck with the white leather lounge. Vaughan would be on that one or one nearby. They would have brought Kimo aboard and presented her to the man who decided the fates of young women he kidnapped, purchased and sold.

Rex refused to let Kimo be one of Vaughan's conquests.

CHAPTER 15

K IMO AWOKE, lying on a soft white carpet in a brightly lit room full of white leather couches and shiny gold accent tables and wall hangings.

"Come on, come on. Wake up already," an impatient voice sounded. "You've caused me enough trouble.

A black, booted foot, incongruous to the stark white furnishings surrounding her, pushed against her side, rolling her onto her back.

A man with thick, salt-and-pepper hair stared down at her, a sneer pulling his lip up on one side.

"Good. I want you to be awake when I bring your friend out. You need to understand and appreciate what happens to those people who cross me."

This had to be Lucien Vaughan—the man behind the deaths of those people in the shipping container. He was also the one who had taken Alana hostage.

Kimo tried to move her arms and legs. They didn't respond to signals from her brain. Though she was awake, she had no control over her body. Then she remembered the needle jab in her neck. The man who'd helped her when she'd stumbled had drugged her.

How long would it take for it to wear off? If she focused, could she work through it and regain the use of her limbs? She concentrated on her fingers and toes, trying to wiggle them. At first, they reacted like her arms and legs, refusing to respond. Then her big toe on her right foot moved.

A door opened somewhere, and booted feet clomped across a hard surface before becoming muffled as if they'd stepped onto the white carpet. Sounds of grunting and cursing came to Kimo, but she couldn't turn her head to see the source.

Then a familiar voice cried out, "Kimo! Oh, sweet Jesus. Not you."

Alana lunged across Kimo, tripped and fell face-first onto the white carpet, unable to break her fall with her hands secured behind her back.

She rolled onto her side, her gaze on Kimo. "Not you, too," she whispered. She wore the soft green bikini she'd had on beneath her wetsuit. The fabric appeared to be spotted with dark stains, which Kimo realized were blood.

Her heart pinched hard in her chest. Her sweet Alana. What had they done to her?

"Now that I have both of you here with your undivided attention," Vaughan said, "we begin your indoctrination. By the time I'm finished with you, you'll be compliant and ready to go to one of my clients in Saudi Arabia, who prefers hula dancers. You do hula, don't you?" He nodded toward someone standing just out of Kimo's view.

A man with black boots leaned over Alana, hooked her under her arms and hauled her to her feet.

She stood with her arms behind her back, her long, beautiful black hair in tangled disarray.

"Dance, Lolita," Vaughan commanded.

Alana glared at the man. "Fuck you." She spit in his face.

Vaughan's face turned a mottled red. He wiped the spittle from his cheek and reached for a long, metal rod with a yellow handle and a black forked tip. He pointed the rod at Alana. "Dance."

When she refused to move, he jabbed the rod at Alana. She cried out and leaped backward.

"Dance," Vaughan commanded.

Alana glared at the man yet still refused to comply. "You're a pathetic excuse for a human," she said in a low, angry voice. "Is your dick so tiny that you have to abuse women to get off? Does it make you feel powerful picking on girls who can't fight back?"

"You'll shut up, or I'll shut you up." He jabbed her again.

She jumped, but bit down hard on her lip, refusing to cry out. "Feel like more of a man yet? You're a pathetic piece of shit."

Oh, Alana, don't make him any madder.

Vaughan hit Alana with the stick and held it on her. When she backed away, he followed until she hit a wall. The cattle prod pressed into her, making her jerk and twitch until she finally cried out.

Kimo forced air past her vocal cords. "Stop." It came out barely above a whisper. She lifted her fingers, though her hands barely moved. "Please. Stop," came out a little louder, capturing Vaughan's attention.

He lowered the cattle prod and advanced on Kimo. "Your friend needs to learn manners. She can't be cursing and calling men names where she's going. They don't tolerate that kind of attitude. They'll cut out her tongue."

He turned back to Alana, where she slumped against the wall. "Is that what you want? Do you want your new owner to cut out your tongue? That will guarantee you won't sling curses at anyone ever again. Maybe I should do him the favor and remove your tongue before I deliver you to him."

"No," Kimo said. "Don't. Hurt. Her."

"No?" Vaughan sneered down at her. "If punishing her doesn't change her behavior, punishing her friend will." He jammed the cattle prod into Kimo's side.

The jolt blasted through her.

Kimo cried out.

"You bastard," Alana yelled. "Leave her alone." Alana pushed away from the wall, bent over and charged at Vaughan like a bull, yelling as she did.

Before she reached him, the man in the black boots caught her around her middle and lifted her off her feet.

She kicked and twisted, but the man holding her was stronger. He held her until she slowed and finally stopped.

When he set her on her feet, Alana dropped to her knees between Kimo and Vaughan. "Don't hurt her."

"What did you say?" he demanded.

Alana glared up at the man and said in a louder voice, "Don't hurt her."

Vaughan moved the cattle prod to his left hand and then backhanded Alana so hard she snapped backward, landing hard on the floor.

"No." Kimo moved her feet, then her legs. Her arms twitched and moved, though not enough to let her stand in the way of the asshole hurting her friend.

"You know, I think it's time to bring back the concept of lashes." To someone else in the room, Vaughan called out, "Bring me my whip."

A door opened and closed.

"Nothing says pain like leather cutting into your skin."

Alana stirred and struggled to sit.

The door behind Vaughan opened again, and footsteps sounded on the tile portions of the lounge floor.

"About time. Hand me the whip." Vaughan held out his hand without looking back at whoever had entered.

A long leather strip snapped through air, striking Vaughan's outstretched hand with a loud sound that cracked the air.

Vaughan jerked his hand back and stared down at the slash across his palm. "Son of a bitch," he said and turned. "I'll have you whipped for that." The man froze.

Kimo managed to turn her head just enough to see who had entered.

Her heart swelled with joy.

Rex stood like Indiana Jones in a wetsuit, his hair wet and slicked back, his feet slightly apart. He held a bull whip down close to his thigh. His arm tensed a moment before he brought the whip up and snapped it toward Vaughan. The leather tip barely touched the man's face, leaving a small, angry slash.

Vaughan cried out and clapped a hand to his cheek. "Don't just stand there," he said to his security guys. "Do something!"

One guard rushed toward him as the other drew his weapon and fired.

At the same moment, the guard closest to Rex lunged for him.

Rex stepped back.

The bullet caught the guard, dropping him to the floor. He didn't move.

Rex dove behind a sofa as the guard kept firing. Kimo held her breath, praying the man missed.

Staying low to the ground, Rex crawled along the back of the sofa. When the guard ran out of ammunition, he dropped the magazine from the handle and reached for another.

Before he could pluck a full magazine from his vest, Rex rose and lunged for him, knocking him to the ground.

Rex landed on top of him. The two men rolled across the carpet, struggling for dominance. Rex was quick and agile. The other man weighed more.

By now, Kimo could move her arms and legs, though they felt heavy and sluggish. She managed to push herself to a sitting position.

Vaughan reached for the cattle prod, snatched it up and hurried toward the men fighting on the floor.

As he passed Kimo, she reached out, snagged his ankle and pulled back as hard as she could.

Vaughan fell. The cattle prod clattered across the floor.

The big guard rolled over, pinning Rex to the ground. Rex flipped the man over his head, scrambled to his feet, pulled a device out of his pocket and touched the man with it before he could move.

The guard jerked and lay still, his eyes wide.

Rex removed the spare magazines from the man's vest, flipped him over and secured his wrists behind his back.

Vaughan was on his feet and running for the door leading deeper into the yacht's interior.

"Rex," Kimo called out. "Get Vaughan before he escapes."

Rex shook his head. "I'm not leaving you. You're not safe."

"I'll never be safe if he gets away."

Rex hesitated a moment. Then he grabbed the guard's weapon, loaded it with a fresh magazine and handed it to Kimo. He dropped the remaining magazine on the carpet next to her. "If anyone comes through that door that you don't recognize, shoot him."

"Be careful," she called after him as she lifted the gun and aimed it at the entrance.

REX BURST through the door into a hallway that stretched the length of the yacht. The door at the end was larger and had more gold embellishments than the others. Though he was positive Vaughan would be in that end suite, Rex checked the doors along the way, opening them one at a time, clearing each room along the way until he came to a stop in front of the most ornate door on the boat.

All he could think was big door, big ego, little penis.

He stood a little to one side as he reached for the handle. When he twisted it, shots rang out. Bullets pierced the wooden door inches away from Rex's shoulder.

Rex pressed his back to the wall until the shooting ceased. Then he jumped in front of the door and slammed it with his heel as hard as he could. As quickly as he'd jumped in front of the door, he plastered his back to the wall again.

More bullets shredded the wood paneling and the gold embellishments. When the firing ceased a second time, Rex waited a second, listening. The creak of hinges made him move in front of the door again. This time, when he kicked the door, it crashed inward. A window on the far side of the room stood open. Vaughan was nowhere to be seen.

Rex ran for the window, glad it was long and wide enough for him to squeeze his body through the opening. It emptied onto the deck on the vessel's side, leading toward the bow. Rex followed the sound of footsteps on metal stairs.

He looked up a stairwell in time to see Vaughan reach the deck with the helipad.

The slow, whomping sound of rotors spinning filled the air, along with the roar of the engine.

Rex's fists clenched.

No. No. No.

Vaughan absolutely could not get away. Kimo's life depended on his capture and indictment.

Rex took the steps two at a time. As he arrived at the top, the chopper blades whipped wind in his face.

Ducking low beneath the whirling blades, Lucien Vaughan climbed into the aircraft.

With only one chance to stop the man, Rex raced forward and flung himself into the chopper, knocking Vaughan flat on his face.

The helicopter started to rise.

Vaughan kicked at Rex in an attempt to get him out. With no intention of staying, Rex slid backward and snagged Vaughan's ankle. When his feet hit the ground, Rex held on, letting the helicopter pull away from the man.

Vaughan dropped onto the helipad, landing hard. He lay so still, he must have been knocked out.

When Rex went to flip him onto his back, Vaughan rolled over and pointed a gun at Rex's chest. "Get up very slowly," he said. "No sudden moves or my finger slips and *boom!* Your father gets to bury his only son."

"You're done, Vaughan." Rex straightened. "Your kidnapping, abusing and trafficking days are over."

"You really have no idea who I am," Vaughan said as he rose carefully and stood facing Rex, the gun still pointed at his chest. "If you turn me in to the authorities, I'll be free within hours."

"It only takes one accomplice with a plea bargain to start the dominoes falling. If Holte is accused of murder, he won't hesitate to point the finger at the guiltiest one of all. And you know the old saying that misery loves company? You might strike the plea bargain yourself to shave some years off your sentence. Either way, there will be no get out of jail free card for you anymore."

Vaughan snorted. "Big talk for a man on the wrong end of a gun barrel."

The helicopter circled and began descending toward the helipad.

"I'm getting on the helicopter. If you try to stop me, your pretty girlfriend will never see you again."

"You aren't going anywhere, Vaughan," Rex said, praying he was right.

"Watch me."

The helicopter lowered until the wheels almost touched the pad.

Vaughan stepped backward until the backs of his legs bumped into the door.

Rex braced himself, preparing to lunge forward

and drag the bastard out again. Before he could make his move, a shot rang out.

Vaughan's legs buckled. He twisted and flung himself toward the open door, his body halfway in, his legs hanging out, unable to push himself further in.

Rex turned to locate the source of the gunfire and found Kimo leaning against a wall, the gun in her hand pointing at the helicopter. She unloaded the magazine into the rotor head.

The helicopter landed hard on the helipad. Vaughan slid out and landed on the ground, blood oozing from his leg.

Rex ducked beneath the rotors as they slowly wound to a stop.

Vaughan leaned over, frantically searching the ground for the gun he'd dropped when he'd fallen to the ground. Rex found it before Vaughan and kicked it out of the man's reach. Then he walked over to pick it up and tuck it into his waistband.

He returned to Vaughan and stared down at the wound on his leg. His first instinct was to let the man bleed out for all the pain and suffering the man had heaped on so many young girls.

Hank's words echoed in his mind, reminding him that Vaughan's testimony would help bring to light the extent of his network and the abusers who'd been getting away with child molestation for years.

He ripped one of Vaughan's sleeves off his arm,

none too gently, and tied it around his leg in a tourniquet to slow the bleeding.

When the pilot finally appeared, Rex secured his wrists behind his back and zip-tied his ankles. Then he made him sit beside Vaughan.

With the deck secure, he hurried over to where Kimo sat with her back to the wall, the gun lying on the deck beside her.

"Are you okay?"

She nodded.

"Alana?"

"I left her with Angel and Devlin. She's bruised, but okay. She'll be happy when she can go home and get a shower."

Boats arrived in Kanapou Bay, filling the decks with every branch of law enforcement, including members of the Maui Police Department.

Rex and Kimo stayed where they were to make certain Vaughan didn't find another way to escape justice.

Hawk and Alana joined them. Alana wore an oversized sweatshirt and sweatpants. Her cheek was still red and starting to turn purple where Vaughan had backhanded her. Despite the bruising, she was smiling. She came to stand beside Kimo and reached for her hand. "I knew you would come for me."

"We would have come sooner if we'd known where to look," Kimo said. "It took a minute to figure it out."

Rex's mouth twisted. "Have you been on the yacht since they captured you?"

Alana nodded. "They locked me in a room down below."

"I was on the yacht last night," Rex said, shaking his head.

Kimo leaned into him, warming his damp wetsuit. "You freed her."

His lips pressed together. "If I'd known sooner…"

"All that matters is that you found me," Alana said. "And Vaughan's going to jail where he belongs."

Kimo nodded and squeezed her friend's hand. "Now that it's over, you can get back to your life and plan your wedding."

Alana snorted. "Or let the wedding planner do it."

"The officer from the Maui Police Department told me that Detective Sykes is MIA," Hawk said. "Sykes was in the office when they received word Lucien Vaughan had been captured and would be charged with murder. When they went to find him to send him out to investigate, he'd disappeared and wasn't answering his cell phone. They have an APB out for him on Maui and at the airport on Oahu."

Men arrived flashing credentials from the FBI, Homeland Security and the local emergency medical service.

Rex frowned as the EMTs loaded Vaughan onto a stretcher and carried him down to the dive deck, where a boat waited to take him to the hospital in Kahului.

"Are you sure they're taking him to the hospital and not to a private plane that will whisk him away to some foreign country?" As slippery as the man was, Rex didn't feel confident letting him out of his sight.

Hawk grinned. "Hank assured me the FBI agent in charge has been tracking Vaughan for a while. Every time he got close to nailing the guy, evidence was lost, and they had nothing. This time, he's making multiple copies of everything and filing it with several agencies besides the FBI, including Interpol, Europol and the UK's National Crime Agency."

"Good. They can't risk the evidence disappearing again," Kimo said.

"Something else we found on the yacht you should know about. Bennett, Logan and Devlin broke into a locked room on a lower deck and found ten girls," Hawk said. "They range in age from twelve to seventeen and hail from various countries."

"Is one of them from Romania?" Rex asked.

Hawk nodded. "As a matter of fact, yes."

Rex tightened the arm he'd had around Kimo's waist. "She's fourteen." He shook his head. "Men like Vaughan need to rot in hell."

Hawk nodded. "Yes, they do. In the meantime, the girls are being loaded onto a boat to be transported to Oahu, where they'll get the care they need. For now, JD is waiting to take us back to Maui, unless you want to ride in the police boat or the charter the FBI and HSI folks arrived in."

Kimo lifted Alana's and Rex's hands. "I want to go wherever these two go."

Alana gave her a crooked smile. "If it's all the same to you, I'd rather not get wet on the way back."

"Since they're heading back the soonest, the FBI charter boat, it is then," Hawk said.

The ride back to Maui on the charter boat seemed to last forever. The RHIB had moved a lot faster and handled the waves better.

The wind felt good on his cheeks, and the rain held off. In fact, the sea seemed a little calmer. At least, it felt like it was. Then again, they weren't wearing their scuba gear and hanging onto an inflatable boat being splashed with every wave the craft hit.

Rex counted the minutes until he could be alone with Kimo again. Now that Vaughan was in custody, Kimo wouldn't need protection. Rex would give the disk to the FBI agent Hank Patterson had recommended after he and Kimo had a chance to review it and make sure there truly was evidence captured on it.

The FBI agent had assured him that if the images were what they thought they were, the disk would be used in the case against Holte, Vaughan and all the people involved in handling the shipping container filled with young girls.

Leilani met them at Maalaea Harbor in her SUV. Angel settled in the passenger seat while Rex, Kimo and Alana climbed into the back.

Leilani drove to Lahaina Harbor, where Rex and Kimo transferred into Rex's truck. They would meet at Leilani and Angel's house in Lahaina for a meal and to decompress.

They sat outside in the shade, surrounded by bougainvillea, hibiscus and two plumeria saplings. After three years waiting and building, Leilani and Angel had moved into the home they'd had constructed in the wake of the fires that had devastated the little town of Lahaina. Like the other residents who'd survived, they chose to rebuild rather than leave Maui. The island was their home. No other place on earth would compare.

Rex had never seen Angel so happy. If *Angel* could find the love of his life, why couldn't he?

As the sun crept toward the horizon, Kimo yawned and stretched. She crossed to where Alana leaned back on a lounge chair, soaking up the last rays before dark.

She bent to hug her friend and pressed a kiss to her cheek. "I'm glad you're back."

Alana caught her hand. "Me, too. And you don't have to worry whether or not I'll dive with you again. I'll go."

"You won't be afraid?" Kimo sighed. "Hell, I'll be looking over my shoulder for months to come."

Kimo glanced across at Rex. "I'm ready to go when you are."

He nodded. "I'm ready."

They said their goodbyes to Angel, Leilani and Alana and climbed into Rex's truck.

Rex headed for Kahului. "Did you want to go to your place?" he asked.

Kimo's brow furrowed. "Did you want me to go to my place?"

With a sharp glance her way, he said, "No."

Her frown slipping away, Kimo sat back with a sigh. "Then can we go to your little cottage by the beach?"

"I was going to suggest it." He reached for her hand. "I know you don't need a protector anymore, but this assignment was far too short. I haven't had nearly enough time getting to know you."

"I've had enough time," Kimo said.

The rush of disappointment sank to the pit of Rex's belly. "You have?"

She nodded. "I've had enough time to know you're special. Enough time to know I'll never find anyone else quite like you." Kimo squeezed his hand. "Enough time to know I'm falling in love with you."

"When you put it like that," Rex said, "forever will never be enough time with you." He grinned. For a guy who'd avoided commitment like the plague, in the short time they'd been together, he'd fallen hard and fast—with absolutely no regrets.

Kimo grinned back. "Shall we start our forever tonight?"

"I can't think of anything I'd like better. In fact," Rex slowed the truck and pulled it to the side of the road. He reached across the console and pulled her close. "I can't think of anyone I could love more than you."

EPILOGUE

Two months later...

Kimo, along with Leilani, Kiana and Alana's cousin Gina, stood on either side of Alana as she stared at her reflection in the full-length mirror.

"Ah..." The collective sighs of her friends made Alana grace them with a shaky smile that disappeared seconds after appearing on her face.

She'd been jumpy and nervous since she'd woken that morning. While Gina and Kiana had assured it was prewedding jitters and that would pass once the wedding began, Kimo suspected it was more, like potentially cold feet and regret that she hadn't called off the wedding in the first place.

After all that Kimo and Alana had been through

with the Lucien Vaughan takedown, Alana had never been the same.

The only reason the large wedding had moved forward was due to the wedding planner spearheading the event like a general going into battle. Vance had taken the lead with the planner when Alana hadn't been able to force herself to make another choice on linens, table settings or meal choices.

Kimo understood. She found the whole idea of spending tens of thousands of dollars on a wedding to be a colossal waste. When she and Rex married, they would ask one of their friends to officiate, write their own vows and have a party on the beach, surrounded by friends.

Alana would have preferred a similar wedding. Already, the bill was well over thirty thousand dollars, and they hadn't finished paying the photographer, caterer and bartender.

Alana sighed. "I would rather have donated the money spent on this wedding to the young girls Vaughan stole from their families and sold into sexual slavery to some fat, entitled prince who had to buy fake affection because he couldn't inspire it on his own."

"It's almost time," Gina said. "We placed your suitcase by the door to the reception hall. Don't worry. We'll load it into the limousine before you leave for your honeymoon."

"Come on, ladies," Gina said. "They're playing our song. We have an aisle to walk." She hugged Alana. "You're gorgeous. I love you. Break a leg." Then she was out the door, taking all her positive, chaotic energy with her.

Kiana and Leilani both hugged Alana and followed Gina.

Kimo, Alana's Maid of Honor, lingered, worried Alana was having second thoughts. "You know it's not too late to call this off," she said.

Alana laughed and choked on a sob. "Are you kidding? After all the money Vance and I spent on this, I'm walking down the damn aisle. Besides, a hundred guests are waiting out there." She shook her head and squared her shoulders. "I'm just nervous. I've never been married before. It happens to all brides, right?"

Kimo stepped in front of Alana and gripped her shoulders. "Do you love Vance?"

"Why wouldn't I? He's handsome, successful and knows how to help plan a wedding. What more do I need?"

"Do you love him? I knew in less than forty-eight hours that I loved Rex. In your heart, do you feel like he's the right one for you?" She cocked an eyebrow. "Be honest with yourself."

Alana looked away. "I thought I was. Then... all that stuff happened." She waved a hand. "The girls…being held captive. It really changes things. It really changed me."

"Again," Kimo said. "Do you love him?"

"It doesn't matter whether I do or not. I'm getting married today." She lifted her chin and adjusted the front of the strapless wedding gown. "I really don't like this dress."

Kimo laughed. "Then why did you choose it?"

"Kinsey chose it for me. It's uncomfortable, and I have an overwhelming fear of my breasts falling out of the fabric midway down the aisle. I'll flash all the guests before I get it pulled back in place. I'll be mortified for life."

The two women waited in the refectory in the wedding chapel that the wedding planner had chosen for Alana and Vance's May wedding on Maui.

The flowers Kinsley and Vance had chosen were white roses and lilies.

Kimo thought they were better suited for a funeral, not a wedding in Hawaii.

The introduction to the wedding march played, making Alana jump. She laughed shakily. "Guess that's our cue. Thanks for being my Maid of Honor and for walking me down the aisle."

"That's my job," Kimo said. "My other job is to sneak you out the back door if you have second thoughts and realize Vance isn't the man for you. We can run away in the limousine, me driving with you riding shotgun."

Kimo had never thought Vance was right for her friend. He was too concerned about appearances and less concerned about Alana. He'd been in New York when Alana had been kidnapped and had never once contacted any of them.

The whole incident had been over by the time he'd returned. He was barely shocked or concerned. As far as Vance had been concerned, it had never happened.

"So, what do you think?" Kimo forced a smile. "I'll be your Thelma to your Louise."

Tears filled Alana's eyes. She reached out and hugged Kimo so tightly she could barely breathe.

When she straightened, her jaw was set. "I didn't live through captivity to run scared of a little wedding. Vance is a good guy. We'll be happy together. Let's do this."

Short of dragging her friend out the door, Kimo had done all she could to convince her to call off the wedding. Instead, she held out her arm.

Alana hooked her hand through Kimo's elbow and walked out of the anteroom into the church. With the wedding march playing, she started down the long aisle with Kimo at her side, taking it slowly, looking ahead for Vance. He wasn't there yet. Shouldn't he be there?

Halfway down the aisles, the guests started whispering. The groomsmen talked among themselves, and the best man's face paled.

The preacher leaned over to whisper something to the best man. The younger man nodded, took a step backward and darted into the room behind the altar.

Alana slowed, the pianist faltered and the music came to a halt.

The best man came out the door with a note in his hand. His gaze met Alana's as he said, "Vance left with Kinsley. The wedding's off."

The guests gasped as one, all eyes moving to Alana, her hair in an updo, her makeup professionally applied—a perfect bride, a beautiful venue, with guests waiting to hear vows exchanged.

And no groom.

Anger rushed up Kimo's neck into her cheeks. "That rat bastard," she murmured. "I knew he wasn't good enough for you."

Alana stood stiffly, with a smile pasted on her face. "I'm going to turn around and walk back out of here with my head held high. That jerk did me a favor." She made a graceful turn, still holding onto Kimo's arm and marched back down the aisles and out of the church. She entered the reception hall and the dressing room where she'd hung the bright red dress she'd planned on wearing on her honeymoon to Cabo San Lucas. Once in the dressing room with her bridesmaids, they helped her strip off the offensive wedding dress, remove all the pins holding her hair in an updo she hated and helped her into the go-to-hell red dress.

She turned to Gina, her cousin and the only other single woman present besides her. "Gina, I need a wingman."

Gina grinned. "Are we going to tar and feather the missing groom?"

Kimo stared into Alana's determined eyes, and a smile spread across her face. "No, Gina, you and Alana are going to Las Cabos."

Alana nodded. "That's right. No use wasting a good honeymoon on a lying, cheating coward when I can take someone infinitely more interesting and who cares more for me than Vance ever did."

Kimo hugged her friend. "Go. Raise some hell. You deserve to let down your hair and do something crazy. Just don't get thrown in jail or come back pregnant."

Kimo and the bridesmaids grabbed the bags of birdseed and ran out ahead of Gina and Alana.

When they came out of the reception hall, they showered them with birdseed and wished them luck in Cabo.

As Alana and Gina were whisked away in the limousine, Kimo was glad Gina had gone with Alana. They'd have a good time together and enjoy a relaxing vacation Vance had paid for.

Rex came to stand beside her. "Think they'll be all right, two females alone in Mexico?"

Kimo laughed. "They'll be fine. They're going to an all-inclusive hotel. What could possibly go wrong?"

THANK you for reading Kimo's Hero. The Brotherhood Protectors Hawaii Series continues with Alana's Hero. Keep reading for the 1st Chapter.

ALANA'S HERO

BROTHERHOOD PROTECTORS
HAWAII BOOK #9

New York Times & *USA Today*
Bestselling Author

ELLE JAMES

Alana's
HERO
BROTHERHOOD PROTECTORS
BROTHERHOOD PROTECTORS HAWAII
New York Times & USA Today Bestselling Author
ELLE JAMES

CHAPTER 1

PERSISTENT LIGHT KNIFED through the slits of Chase Flannigan's eyelids, bringing him back to consciousness with a jolt. Pain pounded through his temples, his left cheekbone stung and one of his ribs hurt every time he took a breath.

He opened one eye, and immediately closed it. The light was blindingly bright. He couldn't remember the light shining this brightly into his bedroom before. Easing open his eyelid again, he stared up at a ceiling fan with blades in the shape of palm leaves.

What the hell? Must have been a helluva brawl.

Forcing both eyes all the way open, he took in the bright walls of the room, the open window and the sunshine streaming through, and relaxed. Oh, yeah, he wasn't in his room back on Coronado. He was in

Cabo San Lucas, celebrating his separation from the US Navy.

No more deployments to hot-as-hell countries. No more commanders demanding more than he was physically able to give. No more enemy forces shooting at him from hidden locations. For the next week, all he had in front of him was sunshine and sandy beaches.

Despite his hangover, a smile curled his lips.

Yeah, this was the life.

When Chase raised his arm and rested his left hand over his eyes to block the sunlight shining on his face, something cool and hard pressed into his eyelid. Lifting his hand, he glanced at it and found that a bright gold band encircled his ring finger. He never wore rings. Rings were what poor suckers who fell into the marriage trap wore. Too many of his buddies had gone to the dark side of matrimony and now had nagging wives and rug rats climbing their pant legs.

Chase was a diehard, sworn-in-blood bachelor, determined to live his days single, footloose and fancy free. His motto was, *Why settle for one item on the menu when you can sample from the whole buffet?* Not that he did it often.

The gold band on his ring finger had to be a joke. Something his buddy, Trevor Anderson, had slipped on his finger when he was too drunk to care or remember.

A soft moan sounded in the bed beside him.

Chase sucked in a sharp breath and then rocketed into self-defense mode. He rolled over and straddled the intruder in his bed, pinning slender wrists to the mattress.

Wide blue eyes stared up at him from the flushed face of a beautifully tousled blonde.

Beautiful or not, she was a stranger in his bed. "Who the hell are you, and what are you doing in my bed?"

She struggled to free her hands, her naked body bucking beneath his. "Let go of me before I scream," she demanded.

In her fight to free herself, the sheets shifted lower, exposing bare breasts to the cool, air-conditioned room. The rosy tips knotted into hard little buds.

Chase's groin tightened, his cock stiffening where it rubbed against the soft curls over her sex. He liked the way she felt beneath him, but he still had no memory of why she was there. "I'll let go of you when you tell me who you are and why you're in my room?"

"*Your* room? This is *my* room. And you better get out before I call the police." She bucked again, the movement making him even harder.

"Not your room, lady. And I'm losing patience." *And control.* If he didn't get some answers soon, he'd embarrass himself with a full-blown hard-on.

Her gaze travelled down his torso to his groin, and she gasped. "You're naked!"

"Darlin', in case you haven't noticed…so are you." He glared down at her, and then swept her body with a pointed stare. "I don't remember inviting you into my room last night."

"What are you talking about? I didn't invite you into *my* room." She tugged at her wrists. "Now, get out before I scream the house down." The woman drew in a deep breath.

Before she could let it out in a nail-driving screech sure to split his hungover head in two, Chase sealed her mouth with his.

At first, she stiffened, her lips drawing into a tight line beneath his. When he started to lift his head, she opened her mouth again to let out that scream.

Chase clamped his mouth over hers again and thrust his tongue between her parted teeth, praying she didn't bite down hard.

He treated her to one of his best kisses, one normally reserved for the fortunate women who made it past the wining and dining. Women he ultimately made love to.

By the time he lifted his head, the woman lay still, her eyelids slightly closed, and her lips parted as if waiting for more.

"Now, can we start over?" he whispered, trailing a path of kisses along her jaw to her earlobe. "I'm Chase. And you are?"

"I'm..." she started, her mouth curving into a sweet smile, then *bam*, "...being held hostage!" she yelled at the top of her voice.

He didn't want to do it, but he had to. Quickly as he could, he bent and kissed her again, swallowing the words she was spewing from her luscious, full lips.

When she quieted down, he raised his head slightly. "Look, I'll quit kissing you, if you'll quit screaming. I'm not here to rape you. I just want answers."

"You already know why I'm here," she said. "Obviously, you gave me some kind of date-rape drug." Her gaze shot to her nakedness. "Otherwise, I wouldn't be lying in this bed naked with a complete stranger. Please," she said, "let me go. I won't tell anyone, I promise. Just let me go."

"I told you, I'm not going to hurt you," he assured her. "And I don't have to rape the women I make love to. They usually come willingly."

"See?" she said. "You must have given me some kind of drug. I wouldn't have come willingly with a stranger. Oh, my God. Did we...did we..."

"Make love, have sex, get funky?" Chase quipped. He tilted toward the waste basket near the nightstand. "Based on the condoms in the trash, I'd say it was a distinct possibility." Straightening to stare down at her again, he said, "I reiterate, I don't rape women. You had to have been a willing participant for there to be more than one condom in there. For the record, there are two."

"Oh, you're disgusting. Please, let me go." She tried again to move her arms.

"I'm going to let go of your wrists, so long as you promise not to slug me." He frowned, wondering if it was a good idea to release her. She could have been the one who'd given him the bruised cheek and rib, and she looked mad enough to do damage to him. Since he was naked, she could really hurt him. "Promise?"

She nodded her head.

He let go of her left wrist.

She brought her hand up to cover her breast.

The sunlight shining through the window glanced off something bright on her ring finger.

"Good God, woman. You're married," Chase exclaimed, appalled that her presence in his bed went against one of his golden rules. *Never bed a married woman.* He leaped off her and the bed and stood a couple feet away, his hands held up in surrender. "I don't know how you got into my room, but *I* don't sleep with married women."

"*Married?*" She glanced at his hand and yanked the sheet up to cover her nakedness. "*I'm* not the married one here. *You* are." She pointed to his ring finger. "You lying bastard. I pity the woman who married you. She has to have shit for brains." Tucking the sheet firmly around her, the woman eased out of the bed. "Where have you put my clothes? Is that your game? Keeping me naked in your room because I can't go running down the hallway in the nude?" She poked a finger at him. "Well, I have news for you, buddy. I don't care if I have to run naked through town. I'm not staying here. You can't keep me, and as soon as I can, I'm turning you in to the authorities."

Chase lifted a bright red dress off the floor and held it up. "This belong to you?"

"My dress!" She grabbed for the dress and held it against her chest. Then her gaze shot to the dresser where a pair of stilettos had landed. She marched over to the dresser, snatched the shoes into her hand and stared down at the paper beneath them. "What the hell?" She dropped the shoes and grabbed the paper. "No, no, no. It can't be. What the hell did you give me last night?" She shoved the paper into Chase's face and demanded, "Tell me this is some sort of sick joke."

He took the document from her hand and glanced down at the words. They were written in Spanish with the English translation beneath. The paper was thick parchment with fancy scrollwork designs on the border. At the top of the page, it read *Acta de Matrimonio,* and beneath it, in English, were the words, Marriage Certificate.

Chase's heart plunged to the pit of his belly as he skimmed the Spanish to find the signature scrawled at the bottom of the page: *Chase Flannigan.* Beside his name in neatly written cursive was the name, *Alana Neal.*

He looked at the ring on his finger, and then glanced at her.

She stood with what appeared to be a photograph in her hand, staring down at the image, her face blanching a startling shade of white. Then she looked to him. "We're married?" Her finger pointed from him back to herself, wrapped in the sheet. "You and me? Married?"

With the proof in his hand, Chase had a hard time refuting her statement. He ran his free hand through his hair. "I don't remember signing this."

She looked over his shoulder at the document. "Is that your signature?"

He nodded. "Looks like it." He jabbed his finger at the name Alana Neal. "Is that yours?"

She closed her eyes. "I'm not believing this. It can't be." She spun, dropped the sheet and slipped the dress over her shoulders. "Whatever the hell happened last night...*didn't,* as far as I'm concerned."

"What do you want me to do about this?" He held up the marriage certificate.

"Tear it up. It didn't happen. You and I are *not* married. No way. No how." She snatched her heels off the floor, marched for the door and held it open. "Get out of my room."

He shook his head. "I can't."

"You sure as hell can." She waved her shoes at the hallway. "Go. Now."

"Ms. Neal…Alana, this is my room."

"If this was your room…" Leaving the door open, she marched to the closet and flung open the door, "Why are my clothes in…" Her gaze took in the crisp white, men's shirt and dark trousers hanging neatly beside a pair of jeans and one of the polo shirts his buddy Trevor said he'd need to fit in with the clientele at the all-inclusive resort. "Where the hell is my suitcase?" She ducked her head into the shallow closet as if searching for a hidden compartment. As she straightened, she pressed a hand to her forehead and swayed. "My head feels like steel wool, and I think I'm going to throw up." She pinched the bridge of her nose and glared at him. "What have you done with my things?"

"Listen to me," he said as slowly and as clearly as he could. "This. Is. Not. Your. Room."

"Yes, it is. It says so right on the door. Room 336." She crossed to the door and pointed at the numbers on the door.

"That's 326, not 336." He leaned out the door and jerked his thumb toward the opposite end of the hallway. "Your room is down there."

She frowned, stared at the numbers, blinked and stared again. With a huff, she whirled and searched the room, her gaze landing on the dresser in his room. "If this isn't my room, is that my room key?"

Chase retrieved the key card from the dresser and ran it over the locking mechanism on the door. The light turned red. He tried again. The light blinked red. "I guess, it is."

She snatched the key from him and marched down the hallway, muttering, "I'm not married. I didn't come to Cabo to get married. This is not happening. It's all one horrible, horrible nightmare. Gina!"

The woman was spitting fire, and Chase found it strangely charming. The marriage certificate still in his hand, he followed, telling himself he wasn't interested, but needed to resolve this little matter of their marriage. "This appears to be a legally binding document. We can't just tear it up," he called out after her.

As much as Chase abhorred the institution of marriage, he kind of liked torturing Alana with the idea she might be legally bound to him in holy matrimony. This thought gave him an inordinate amount of pleasure. He followed her to room 336. "We can't just tear up this certificate. It's stamped, and a copy is probably stored in some archive somewhere."

"We sure as hell can," she called over her shoulder. "What happens in these kinds of places stays in these places. That certificate won't hold up in the US courts. I'm a US citizen, subject to the US court system. I'm not married." She waved her key card over the door lock, and the light turned green. Alana pushed into the suite. "Gina!" Without waiting for a response, she charged across the room like a bull toward a matador's red cape and flung open a door. "Gina! What the hell happened last night?"

A startled squeal sounded from the bed. "Geez, woman. Haven't you ever heard of knocking?"

READ MORE OF ALANA'S HERO
Alana's Hero

ABOUT THE AUTHOR

ELLE JAMES also writing as MYLA JACKSON is a *New York Times* and *USA Today* Bestselling author of books including cowboys, intrigues and paranormal adventures that keep her readers on the edges of their seats. When she's not at her computer, she's traveling, snow skiing, boating, or riding her ATV, dreaming up new stories. Learn more about Elle James at www.ellejames.com

Website | Facebook | Twitter | GoodReads | Newsletter | BookBub | Amazon

Or visit her alter ego Myla Jackson at
mylajackson.com
Website | Facebook | Twitter | Newsletter

Follow Me!
www.ellejames.com
ellejamesauthor@gmail.com

ALSO BY ELLE JAMES

Stealth Operations Specialists Series

Saint Nick (#1)

Rogue (#2)

Crusher (#3)

Draco (#4)

A Killer Series

Chilled (#1)

Scorched (#2)

Erased (#3)

Brotherhood Protectors International

Athens Affair (#1)

Belgian Betrayal (#2)

Croatia Collateral (#3)

Dublin Debacle (#4)

Edinburgh Escape (#5)

France Face-Off (#6)

Brotherhood Protectors Hawaii

Kalea's Hero (#1)

Leilani's Hero (#2)

Kiana's Hero (#3)

Casey's Hero (#4)

Maliea's Hero (#5)

Emi's Hero (#6)

Sachie's Hero (#7)

Kimo's Hero (#8)

Alana's Hero (#9)

Bayou Brotherhood Protectors

Remy (#1)

Gerard (#2)

Lucas (#3)

Beau (#4)

Rafael (#5)

Valentin (#6)

Landry (#7)

Simon (#8)

Maurice (#9)

Xavier (#10)

Jacques (#11)

Papa Noel (#12)

Koolaroo Ranch Series

with Kendall Talbot

Outback Secrets (#1)

Outback Escape (#2)

Outback Obsession (#3)

Outback Justice (#4)

Everglades Overwatch Series

with Jen Talty

Secrets in Calusa Cove

Pirates in Calusa Cove

Murder in Calusa Cove

Betrayal in Calusa Cove

Raven's Cliff Series

with Kris Norris

Raven's Watch (#1)

Raven's Claw (#2)

Raven's Nest (#3)

Raven's Curse (#4)

Brotherhood Protectors Yellowstone

Saving Kyla (#1)

Saving Chelsea (#2)

Saving Amanda (#3)

Saving Liliana (#4)

Saving Breely (#5)

Saving Savvie (#6)

Saving Jenna (#7)

Montana Ranger's Wedding Vow (#8)

Montana SEAL Undercover Daddy (#9)

Cape Cod SEAL Rescue (#10)

Montana SEAL Friendly Fire (#11)

Montana SEAL's Mail-Order Bride (#12)

SEAL Justice (#13)

Ranger Creed (#14)

Delta Force Rescue (#15)

Dog Days of Christmas (#16)

Montana Rescue (#17)

Montana Ranger Returns (#18)

Brotherhood Protectors Boxed Set 1

Brotherhood Protectors Boxed Set 2

Brotherhood Protectors Boxed Set 3

Brotherhood Protectors Boxed Set 4

Brotherhood Protectors Boxed Set 5

Brotherhood Protectors Boxed Set 6

Iron Horse Legacy

Soldier's Duty (#1)

Ranger's Baby (#2)

Marine's Promise (#3)

SEAL's Vow (#4)

Warrior's Resolve (#5)

Drake (#6)

Grimm (#7)

Murdock (#8)

Utah (#9)

Judge (#10)

Delta Force Strong

Ivy's Delta (Delta Force 3 Crossover)

Breaking Silence (#1)

Breaking Rules (#2)

Breaking Away (#3)

Breaking Free (#4)

Breaking Hearts (#5)

Breaking Ties (#6)

Breaking Point (#7)

Breaking Dawn (#8)

Breaking Promises (#9)

Hearts & Heroes Series

Wyatt's War (#1)

Mack's Witness (#2)

Ronin's Return (#3)

Sam's Surrender (#4)

Hellfire Series

Hellfire, Texas (#1)

Justice Burning (#2)

Smoldering Desire (#3)

Hellfire in High Heels (#4)

Playing With Fire (#5)

Up in Flames (#6)

Total Meltdown (#7)

Take No Prisoners Series

SEAL's Honor (#1)

SEAL'S Desire (#2)

SEAL's Embrace (#3)

SEAL's Obsession (#4)

SEAL's Proposal (#5)

SEAL's Seduction (#6)

SEAL'S Defiance (#7)

SEAL's Deception (#8)

SEAL's Deliverance (#9)

SEAL's Ultimate Challenge (#10)

Cajun Magic Mystery Series

Voodoo on the Bayou (#1)

Voodoo for Two (#2)

Deja Voodoo (#3)

Texas Billionaire Club

Tarzan & Janine (#1)

Something To Talk About (#2)

Who's Your Daddy (#3)

Love & War (#4)

Billionaire Online Dating Service

The Billionaire Husband Test (#1)

The Billionaire Cinderella Test (#2)

The Billionaire Bride Test (#3)

The Billionaire Daddy Test (#4)

The Billionaire Matchmaker Test (#5)

The Billionaire Glitch Date (#6)

The Outriders

Homicide at Whiskey Gulch (#1)

Hideout at Whiskey Gulch (#2)

Held Hostage at Whiskey Gulch (#3)

Setup at Whiskey Gulch (#4)

Missing Witness at Whiskey Gulch (#5)

Cowboy Justice at Whiskey Gulch (#6)

Boys Behaving Badly Anthologies

Rogues (#1)

Blue Collar (#2)

Pirates (#3)

Stranded (#4)

First Responder (#5)

Cowboys (#6)

Silver Soldiers (#7)

Secret Identities (#8)

Warrior's Conquest

Enslaved by the Viking Short Story

Conquests

Smokin' Hot Firemen

Protecting the Colton Bride

Protecting the Colton Bride & Colton's Cowboy Code

Heir to Murder

Secret Service Rescue

High Octane Heroes

Haunted

Engaged with the Boss

Cowboy Brigade

An Unexpected Clue

Under Suspicion, With Child

Texas-Size Secrets